HEARTS & CRAFTS

Also by
Lisa Papademetriou:

HEARTS & CRAFTS

#2: Pet Project

Lisa Papademetriou

SCHOLASTIC INC.

This book is dedicated to Amanda Maciel,
who always puts her heart into the craft.

ISBN 978-1-338-60307-1

10 9 8 7 6 5 4 3 2 1   22 23 24 25 26

Printed in the U.S.A.   40

First printing 2022

Book design by Yaffa Jaskoll and Keirsten Geise

CHAPTER ONE

"Oh, turkey, I forgot the dessert," Mom said the minute we pulled up to my aunt's brown ranch-style house.

"We were supposed to bring dessert?" I looked over my shoulder at the backseat, in case there was a cake or something that I had forgotten about.

Mom sighed and glanced doubtfully at me. "Should we head over to Tart Café to get a pie?"

"That's ten minutes away," I pointed out. My aunt lives in a place I call "the middle of nowhere" and that Mom calls "a more rural environment." It's only a short drive from the center of town, but there's also an actual farm at the end of Aunt Goldie's road. Sometimes the breeze smells like wet cow and fertilizer . . . in a good, tangy way. "We'll be twenty minutes late if we get dessert," I said. "And we're already here. Aunt Goldie doesn't care that much about pie."

Mom still looked stressed, so I added, "Everyone forgets stuff, Mom." I very nicely did not point out that she had been forgetting stuff right and left lately.

"It's just . . . *work*," she said. Her hands gripped the steering wheel even though the car was parked. "It's giving me brain fog."

I nodded. Mom started a new job a few weeks ago, and then a bigger company bought her company. All of a sudden, she had a bunch of new responsibilities. I knew she was still trying to figure everything out. "They should pay you more money," I said.

Those words seemed to snap her back to the present. Mom reached for the door handle, pushed open the car door, and smiled at me. "They're still reorganizing everything to make two companies into one big one. I might end up with a different job; I might even end up with a promotion."

"They should have promoted you already!" I insisted.

Mom laughed. "Mackenzie, I love your confidence. But I've been in this job for less than two months. We'll see what happens, okay?"

I grunted in a way that meant *I'm right and you know it* as we both stepped out of the car and headed toward my aunt's side door. Only people promoting political candidates or trying to sell cookies ever showed up at the front entrance, so she never answered it.

I could smell Aunt Goldie's famous roast beef when I knocked, and was met with the sound of two sharp barks, and then scrambling toenails clicking across the wood floor.

"Sounds like she has a visitor," I said, and a moment later we heard my aunt say, "Buster, now sit. Okay, good boy." Then she pulled open the door, smiling hugely, her blonde hair in a messy bun at the base of her neck. She was wearing a white V-neck shirt and faded jeans. Next to her was a brown-black-and-white dog with bright eyes and a bit of gray at his muzzle.

"Who's this?" I cried as Mom said, "What a cutie!"

The dog spotted something behind me and stood up suddenly.

"Close the—" Goldie cried, but the dog—Buster, I assumed—had already darted out the side door. A squirrel streaked across the driveway and bounded up a tree. Buster was instantly standing at the roots, barking furiously up at a branch and the fiercely chattering squirrel. Goldie sighed. "Yeah, we're still working on that."

"It's going great," Mom teased.

"It isn't easy to catch Buster once he spots a squirrel," Goldie admitted as she reached for a leash on the peg by the door. "He's a Jack Russell terrier—they're fast."

I hurried into the kitchen and pulled a tiny piece of beef from the roast. "Okay?" I asked as I held it up.

"He'll be your best friend," Goldie said, and I went outside calling, "Buster!"

He glanced over at me and caught a whiff of the beef. He glanced back up at the squirrel, almost like he was saying, *Catch you later*, then turned toward me and plopped into a sit, waiting for his treat. "He's trained," I said as I held out the treat. As he chewed, I gently took hold of his collar.

"Somewhat." Goldie joined us and clicked on the leash. "He's housebroken and knows how to sit. But he's a little rambunctious."

"How old is he?" Mom asked as her sister guided Buster back inside and removed the leash. I shut the door and we all headed into the kitchen.

"He's nine." Goldie washed her hands and then headed to the counter to slice the roast beef. "His owner passed away, and her daughter inherited him. She brought him in because his fur had started falling out. Anyway, I asked a few questions and it turned out that she had been keeping him in the garage because she was allergic to him. She took him out a couple of times a day but that was it."

Mom bent down to scratch Buster behind the ears. He stood up, his butt wiggling with every wag of his stumpy tail.

"So he's yours now?" I looked over at Buster, who was sitting again, paying very careful attention to the plates as Aunt Goldie filled them with mashed potatoes, gravy, green beans, and roast beef. His little tail wiggled from side to side against the floor.

"No—I'm not home enough to care for a dog," Aunt Goldie said. "He needs to socialize and explore. I think he's losing his fur because he was stressed out from being alone. But I talked the woman into surrendering Buster—which wasn't that hard to do. She seemed really relieved when I promised I'd take him to the shelter and see personally that he got a good home. I just wanted to observe him and make sure he didn't have any more medical issues before I brought him over, which I'll do Monday." She placed the plates on the table and gestured for us to sit.

All my aunt's furniture looks like it was found by the side of the road, which it was. Aunt Goldie always says that she hates the idea of nice furniture because she has too many houseguests. (The houseguests are all animals.) I chose the sturdiest-looking chair and drew the paper towel napkin across my lap as Goldie directed Buster to his bed and put up a doggie playpen around him. He rested his chin on the edge of the pillow and looked up at us with big eyes.

"What a horrible person," I said, thinking about the woman who had kept him in her garage.

"She felt terrible about it." Aunt Goldie slipped into her seat. "She knew it wasn't a good situation, but she felt she owed it to her mom to try."

"But poor Buster," I insisted.

"Sometimes people can't think straight when they lose someone," Mom said gently. "Her mother had died, after all."

I huffed out a breath. I knew Mom was right, but did she really always have to be so *nice* and *understanding* all the time? Buster had been locked in a garage! And he was clearly such a good dog.

"I'm sure he'll find a family who loves him," Mom added.

"It can be hard to place a senior dog, but I'm sure we'll find someone." Aunt Goldie smiled.

"He's a sweetie," Mom agreed. "Someone would be lucky to have him."

As if he realized we were talking about him, Buster sat up, his ears pricked, with the tips flopping over. Then he rose onto his haunches, with his front paws dangling in a begging pose, which made us all laugh.

"You didn't tell me he could do that!" I cried.

"I didn't know! I guess he wants some more roast beef," Aunt Goldie said. "I'll give him a little more later.

"You have to wait," she told Buster, who turned in a circle and settled back onto his bed.

We finished dinner, which was excellent, as always. To be clear, my aunt only knows how to make one fancy meal: the one we just ate. We eat that whenever we come over, which is about once every three months. Aunt Goldie doesn't really care about cooking—she's too busy working as a vet tech, volunteering at the shelter, and studying to be a veterinarian. It's a bummer that she's so busy these days because she's an awesome aunt. She's crazy about amusement parks and fairs and takes me on all the rides, even the scary, stomach-dropping ones that Mom can barely look at. She knows every waterfall in the area, and sometimes we go for hikes and end up splashing in the water. Goldie also loves action movies, and she used to take me to all the big opening weekends. We haven't done any of those things lately, though. The only consolation is that I know she misses it all as much as I do.

After dinner, Goldie opened Buster's pen and let him do a few tricks for treats. He showed us that he knew how to lie down and roll over. Mom got him to hop up on his hind feet and congratulated him with a treat and a hug. He gave her a big lick on the cheek, which made her giggle.

Then we played Uno, and I won the most games, as usual, mostly because my mom can never remember to say "Uno" and my aunt never pays attention to anyone's cards but her own.

"One more round?" I asked, shuffling the deck.

"Well, I have to play," Mom said. "I can't get up." She smiled down at Buster, who had settled into her lap and was snoring softly. She ran her hand gently over his back. "What a good boy."

"Pets are scientifically proven to be relaxing," Aunt

Goldie said as I handed her the deck to deal the cards.

"Maybe we should bring him home with us," I suggested.

"Mackenzie, we can't get a dog," Mom said, patting Buster. "I work too much."

"I meant for the weekend." I picked up my cards, which included two Draw Fours. "We can bring him to the shelter on Monday for Aunt Goldie."

"Wow, do you think you could do that?" Goldie asked. "I told my study group to go ahead without me because I didn't want to leave Buster alone, but it would be really great if I could meet up with them." She looked over at my mom, who patted Buster's head.

This is just what Mom needs! I realized. She seemed more relaxed than she had in three weeks. Besides, it was Friday— we could take Buster to the park on Saturday and maybe even down to the river on Sunday.

"We could have a chill weekend, just going to the park and stuff," I pointed out. "And you'll have someone to sit next to you on the couch while you watch your cheesy romance movies." She hesitated, so I added, "Besides, we'd be helping Aunt Goldie."

Mom looked at her little sister and rolled her eyes.

My aunt winked at me. "An offer you can't refuse, right, Allison?" Goldie's eyes sparkled.

I smiled down at the cards in my hand. I had already won this round, and I knew it.

"What's going on?" I asked as Mom pulled into our driveway.

Limp garbage lay dusted across the side lawn, and our neighbor Zane was collecting it into a fresh bag. His black hair was its usual tousled tangle and his black eyes crinkled into a smile over the bandana he'd pulled up over his nose, Jesse James–style. He was also wearing yellow rubber gloves, which—with his usual T-shirt and jeans—gave the whole outfit a real high-fashion vibe.

We got out of the car and I let Buster hop out of the backseat. It was lucky I had a good hold on his leash because he was very interested in sniffing out the situation.

"Raccoons again?" Mom asked as she walked over to give Zane a kiss on the cheek.

"I scared them off, but they love our trash cans. You

definitely don't want to come too close," Zane said, just as a putrid whiff of eau-du-garbage wafted by. He pointed to the bandana. "It's a bit funky."

I started breathing through my mouth.

In addition to living next door in our duplex, Zane is also Mom's kind-of-sort-of boyfriend. I call him that because a couple of weeks ago I asked if he and my mom were boyfriend and girlfriend, and he said, "Sort of," while she said, "No." Then they looked at each other, and Zane said, "Oh, no, I guess," while my mom said, "Maybe kind of, then." So I was like, "That was pretty smooth," and they both laughed and then Zane took my mom's hand and it was all cute enough to make a person throw up. I mean, which of these three people is in middle school, again?

Buster had his nose to the ground and was sniffing intensely. "Someone thinks it smells great," I said.

"Did you guys go out and get a dog?" Zane asked.

"Buster is a houseguest," Mom explained. "For the weekend."

"Ah."

"Do you want to pet him?" I asked.

Zane held up his trash bag and said, "Maybe later." But

Buster wanted an introduction and came over to sniff at Zane's shoe. "What's he doing?"

"Getting to know your foot," I explained.

"Hm," Zane said. His face was covered by the bandana, so I couldn't really read his expression, but his voice didn't seem terribly enthusiastic.

"You're not a dog person?" Mom asked. She sounded surprised.

"I just . . . didn't grow up with them," Zane explained. "We didn't come to the United States until I was in middle school, and in Pakistan, people don't usually have dogs."

"There are no dogs in Pakistan?" I repeated. That seemed bizarre.

"No, there are dogs, of course. But people don't usually keep them as pets, you know, in the house. Like people do here. I'm not really a pet guy; I just never had one."

"Dogs are great!" I said. "And you'll love Buster."

Zane laughed. "Is that a command?"

That made me giggle. I guess it had sounded a little bossy. "It's a prediction."

"Oh, and speaking of predictions," Zane said, "you might hear from my niece—"

My phone buzzed. When I pulled it from my back pocket, I saw that Sheera was FaceTiming me. "Wow, you're good at that," I told Zane.

He lifted his thick eyebrows knowingly and I touched the screen, wondering what was up.

Sheera's eyes were huge behind her purple-framed glasses. "Kenzie!" she cried. "Something terrible is happening!"

I glanced over at Zane, who rolled his eyes.

"Is my uncle there? Is he rolling his eyes?" Sheera demanded.

I turned the phone. "Hi," Zane called, waving a yellow-gloved hand.

"Hi, Sheera," Mom chimed in.

"Hi," Sheera said. "Listen—"

"Wait, wait, can I just introduce you to someone else who's here?" I asked. I pointed the phone down so that Buster was visible. He sniffed at the screen.

"Oh, he's so cute!" Sheera said. "Is he yours?" I explained the situation and Sheera said, "I can't wait to meet him!"

"You can come over this weekend. We'll take him for a walk," I told her. "So what's this big news?"

"Are you ready for this? YASMIN IS COMING TO WARD."

"Your cousin is switching to our school?" I asked. "Why?"

"Because she wants to ruin my life, probably!"

"Do you think she'll throw another flip-flop at you?" I teased.

"More like she'll bad-mouth me and try to steal my friends, like she did in first grade." Sheera fiddled with the edge of her peace-sign-patterned headscarf, then adjusted her glasses.

"We're not in first grade," I pointed out. I glanced over at my mom and Zane, who had finished picking up the trash and setting the overturned garbage bins upright. They gave each other a little wave as Zane went into his half of the duplex, probably to wash his hands and change his clothes. Mom pointed at our door to say that she was going in, and I nodded.

Sheera huffed out a sigh. "Ugh, we'll see."

"At least, *I'm* not in first grade, and nobody is stealing me as your friend," I said. "What are you worried about? Yasmin's going to be the new girl; she's the one who should be worried."

"Hm." Sheera narrowed her eyes.

"It isn't easy to be the new kid at school," I suggested. "Won't you at least try to be nice to her?"

She tilted her head and rolled her eyes.

"Is that a yes?" I asked.

"Don't make me say it."

"Just tell me you'll try to get along," I told her. "You can't be in a bad mood for the rest of seventh grade."

Scoffing noise. Dramatic sigh. And then a reluctant "Fiiiiiiiine."

"Besides, you might not even run into her; Ward is huge! Right, Buster?" I gave Buster a scratch behind the ears and he wagged. "Listen, I've got to get Buster set up, okay? See you tomorrow?"

"Sounds good." She disappeared from the screen, and Buster and I headed into the house.

"Friends can be very dramatic," I told him as he hopped up the front steps. "That's what's great about dogs—you're drama-free. You're just going to be a nice, relaxing treat for Mom, right, buddy?"

A few weeks before, I'd had an argument with my friends. Johanna and Sheera had both complained that I never ask for help, and I had to admit they were right—and that it sometimes gets me into trouble. So I was working on it. "Which is why *you're* going to be my helper with Mom," I told the little dog.

Buster looked up at me, head cocked as if he were trying to figure out what I was saying. With his ears pricked up and the ends flopped over, he looked like a puppy. *Who wouldn't want a great dog like this?* I wondered. *Someone's going to scoop him up right away.*

"Look at this guy!" Mom said the next day as Buster sat up on his haunches. "I just gave him a little piece of chicken—he loves it!"

"You shouldn't feed him from the table, Mom," I said.

"I didn't." She put her plate in the dishwasher and closed it with a *thunk*. "I gave it to him at the sink."

I wasn't sure that was much better, but Buster wasn't going to be with us long enough to have it make much of a difference. "Hey, Mom, do you think Sheera could spend the night this weekend?"

"Honey, it's already Saturday afternoon! I've still got

some work to do, and we have to take care of Buster, so I don't think it's a good idea." Mom wiped her hands on a kitchen towel, threaded it through the refrigerator handle, then leaned against the counter with her arms folded. "Besides, you know I don't love doing sleepovers unless I know the parents. Because if we have her here, she'll probably want to have you over there . . . It's just always best when the parents know each other a little."

"Well, let's have them over, then. We could have a barbecue or something, for the whole family."

Mom shook her head, then ran her hands through her brown hair. "Not this weekend."

"Next?"

"Maybe. Let me see how work is going, okay? I'll let you know soon."

"Yay!" I said. Sometimes, it's best to just act as if something is happening until it does.

"Now, listen, I have to answer a few emails. And then we can go for a hike by the river with Buster."

"No problem. I took a new book out of the library and I wanted to start it. Come on, Buster!" I made a kissing noise.

Mom grabbed her computer from the table and walked over toward the couch.

Buster looked at me. Then he looked at my mom. He gave me a final glance, like, *Sorry, but this lady hands out chicken*, then trotted after her and leaped onto the couch at her side.

"Hey, buddy," I heard Mom say. "Want to help me write some emails?"

I felt a little jab of jealousy, just a little sliver, like a paper cut. But then I realized that this was a good thing. The perfect thing, in fact. After all, Buster was here to make my mom feel more relaxed, and he was already doing an outstanding job.

DIY: How to Make a Mom Happy

Let me tell you something: We used to have a dog.

This was long ago, back when I was three or four. I don't remember Harpo very well, but Mom says he loved me. She has photos of us curled up together when I was a baby. We never really knew what breed of dog he was, but he was small and very fluffy, probably part poodle, part Chihuahua or something.

"My first baby," Mom always says when she talks about Harpo, and I know she's joking but also kind of not. Harpo was her dog even before she met my dad. Aunt Goldie says Harpo is the reason she decided to become a vet because she was so sad when Harpo got cancer.

Mom keeps four photos on her bureau. One is my school photo, which she updates every year. The one next to it is a picture of me, Poppy, and Grannynanny, my grandmother who passed away a few years ago. One is a photo of my mom when she was about five, a toddler Aunt Goldie, and their parents, my other grandparents. And the last is a photo of Harpo.

My dad was never really a dog guy. I guess he liked Harpo, but Harpo was my mom's dog.

Anyway, I know Mom loved Harpo and he made her happy.

Dogs are happy things.

And studies show that petting a dog can lower stress and make you feel happier, which was exactly what Mom needed now.

So I was glad that Buster was staying with us, even if it was just for a weekend.

CHAPTER TWO

"Zee-Zee!" Johanna waved from her seat at the edge of the second planter and called, "What's this about getting a dog?"

I waved back and hurried over to where she was sitting with Sheera in our usual meeting spot. There are five large, concrete planters in front of the side entrance to Ward Middle School. Each holds a tree and has edges wide enough to sit on. If we get to school early enough, Johanna, Sheera, and I always try to grab the second one from the door so we can hang out until the first bell rings.

"I've been telling her about Buster," Sheera explained.

"Picture?" Johanna asked, her hazel eyes shining.

I slid onto the planter beside her and pulled out my phone. "He's heading over to the shelter later," I explained as I scrolled. Then I played her a couple of short videos: Buster jumping in a pile of yellow leaves and dragging them all over the place, Buster licking my mom's foot and making her laugh, Buster catching a tossed treat in midair. I ended just as the bell rang by clicking on my favorite photo: me hugging Buster while he licked my cheek.

"He's adorable!" Johanna gushed.

"Oh, ew," Sheera said.

"Relax, I washed my face right after," I told her.

Sheera waved her hand toward the drop-off circle. "No, I mean . . ."

A curvy girl with waist-length black hair and the same eyes as Sheera's was walking toward us. She wore a flowered maxi dress with a stylish cropped jean jacket, and her nails were done, all of which easily made her the best-dressed girl in school.

"Is that—" I started.

"That's her," Sheera whispered as Yasmin smiled and waved.

"What am I missing?" Johanna asked.

"You're about to witness Sheera being super nice to a new kid," I said cheerfully.

Johanna shot a suspicious glance toward Sheera, who

snorted softly, then waved to Yasmin and called, "Hey! Happy first day of school."

"Very good," I whispered. "Keep it up!"

"Don't push it," Sheera snapped under her breath.

"Hi!" Yasmin called as she jogged the last few yards toward us. She wrapped Sheera in a warm hug and rocked back and forth enthusiastically. Sheera stood there stiffly, her arms locked against her sides and her face locked in an expression roughly the same as someone who'd been enveloped by a python. "I'm so glad I found you right away!" Yasmin gushed, releasing Sheera from the hug. She brushed a few loose strands of black hair from her face and flashed a brilliant smile toward me and Johanna. "Are these your friends?"

"Uh, yeah." Sheera gestured to me, then Johanna, and introduced us to her cousin.

"Great to meet you! Maybe you can help me find my classes. Oh! And I have this thing that my brother said I should give to the librarian." She dug around in her backpack and pulled out a tiny blue shirt. It had a picture of our mascot—a husky—on the front.

Johanna lifted her eyebrows doubtfully. "Um . . . I'm not sure that's Mr. Dodd's size."

Yasmin's soft brown eyes grew wide, and she let out a musical laugh. "Oh, it's not for him," she explained. She turned the shirt around so we could see the back. It read SCOUT over a large athletic number 01. "It's for the therapy dog! I hear kids read to him sometimes. I thought it would be cute if he had a little school shirt."

"That's the cutest!" I said. "Where did you get it?"

"Oh, my mom owns this store," Yasmin said, waving her hand as if it was no big deal. "We sell dog stuff. I just took a plain shirt and then put a design on transfer paper."

"You *made* it?" I asked, looking at the shirt again. It was really adorable—I made a mental note to have Yasmin show me how she did it.

"Oh, right, Poochalicious," Johanna chimed in. "Sheera's told us all about it."

"You brought a shirt for a dog?" Sheera sighed. "I doubt Mr. Dodd will even let Scout wear it."

Yasmin shoved the shirt into her bag and her eyes dropped to the phone in my hand. "Oh my goodness, who is that *cutie*? Is he your dog?"

"This is Buster—"

"You should bring him by Poochalicious! I'm there a lot; I can hook you up with some cool stuff."

I heard myself say, "That sounds like fun!" But then I realized my mistake.

Sheera looked at me, one eyebrow raised. "Isn't Buster going back to the shelter today?" she asked.

I felt the heat in my cheeks. "She's right," I said to Yasmin. I'd been so carried away by her energy that I'd completely forgotten that Buster wasn't actually my dog.

Yasmin's full bottom lip stuck out in a pout. "Oh, too bad."

"Yeah, too bad this dog can't get a makeover because he's going to find a home," Sheera put in.

Yasmin looked at her, and her brown eyes flashed like lightning across a dark sky. Then she seemed to catch herself, and said, "You're right." She tossed her hair and the fire in her expression died away, like a fuse that fizzles out. "Maybe the next time you foster a dog," she told me, and I smiled. Then I caught Sheera's expression, and my stomach tightened. She didn't look happy.

"Hello, lovely people of the seventh grade," said a voice as buttery as movie theater popcorn. I turned to find Tariq

Mirza, grinning and holding five stacks of colorful Post-its fanned out like a deck of cards.

"Speaking of hounds," Sheera said. Tariq is Sheera's cousin; Yasmin's brother.

"Ick, Tariq; I told you not to talk to me at school," Yasmin said.

"Who's talking to you?" He leaned across the planter to wave the Post-its under my nose. "Did anyone leave any supplies at home? Sticky notes, mechanical pencils, gel pens?"

"What happened to selling candy?" Johanna asked. "What's with the school supplies?"

Tariq shrugged. "The school banned selling candy. Hey, what's this behind your ear?" he asked, gesturing toward my head and producing something with a flourish. "Why, it's an adorable eraser shaped like a cow! Only a dollar!"

"Listen, Magic Boy, do something useful and make yourself disappear," Yasmin told him.

"All right, all right, I'm going," he said with a smirk. "Just remember, I'm the *cool guy* with the *school supplies*." He waggled his eyebrows as he delivered the rhyme.

Yasmin rolled her eyes. "He's been practicing that in the mirror all weekend." She gave him a little shove, and Tariq headed off toward a tight knot of sixth graders, who greeted him with friendly smiles.

"What an operator," Johanna said. "You've kind of got to admire the guy."

Yasmin tilted her head doubtfully. "Do you?"

"Nope," Sheera said.

Yasmin held up a palm and Sheera slapped it just as the bell rang. I hitched my backpack over my shoulder and took a deep breath as the knot in my stomach loosened. So . . . this was Yasmin. Honestly, she seemed pretty cool—great style, awesome crafting instincts, a love of dogs. I could see myself being friends with her . . . if Sheera could chill out a little and they could figure out a way to get along. For a reason other than mutual annoyance at Tariq, ideally.

Hm, I thought. *Can you ship two people to be friends with each other?* Because I was practically setting sail.

It might take a little work, but I was pretty sure I could make it happen.

A chilly wind blew yellow maple leaves around us as Sheera and I walked Buster along the path from the edge of the lake toward my house after school. The sky overhead was clear, and Buster didn't seem to mind the cold, trotting happily a few feet ahead of us.

"I love how it looks like he's wearing pants," Sheera said, smiling at Buster's brown haunches.

"Pants with a pocket." I pointed at an irregular white patch on his right flank, and Sheera laughed.

"I wish he didn't have to go back to the shelter," she said.

"I know. I'll miss him! We had such a great time together. Even my mom said that she wished he could stay a little longer."

Buster had been a perfect angel all weekend, in fact, spending hours curled up at my mom's feet when we weren't out walking together. Mom really had seemed more relaxed, and I was feeling like a super-genius.

"Aww."

"You should have seen them hanging out. He loves to sit as close as possible to my mom—on her toes, on her lap."

"Cute."

"Besides, if he stayed, I could knit him a sweater."

Sheera shook her head and looked at me over the purple

frames of her glasses. "Mackenzie, not everything involves a craft."

"But he could use a sweater!" I pointed out. "The fur on his chest is patchy, and it's almost winter." I buttoned up my jacket and gave her a meaningful look.

"Someone can *buy* him a sweater."

Sheera and I stopped to let Buster sniff at the base of a bush. He dug at the ground with one paw, then sniffed some more. After a minute, he seemed satisfied and lifted his leg on the spot.

"I guess he had to leave someone a note," Sheera said.

"That's gross."

"No, I'm serious. I read that dogs do that. They pee to say, 'This is my territory,' or whatever."

"Buster?" He looked up at me and cocked his head. "You need to learn to text." I bent down and petted him, and we started along the path again. As we got close to the edge of the park, our conversation turned to the school band. Sheera and I both play the oboe.

"I think we're finally getting it together," Sheera said. "Or we would be, if you could hear the flutes."

"Yeah, but I still don't think I've got that fast part right.

You know the one with the sixteen beats in two measures? How is that supposed to go?" We turned onto the street that led to my house.

Sheera hummed it for me, and when I winced and gestured, she hummed it again more slowly. Then she did it again at the right tempo.

I hummed it back.

"Almost—" She lifted her eyebrows and hummed it again, putting extra emphasis on the part I'd gotten wrong.

"Okay, I get it," I told her. I hummed it back, and she nodded.

"The notation is confusing," she said sympathetically.

"You've got such a good ear," I told her. "I bet you sing well."

She shrugged. "In my room." We were halfway down the street, and I could see my house. But Sheera's eyes were on the house across the street, where my friend Dickens lives.

My duplex is Victorian, with two large bay windows in front—one for each living room, Zane's and ours. But Dickens's house is a small Cape that looks like something out of a storybook. The large maple tree in the front yard was ablaze with orange and yellow leaves under a crown of green, and in his side yard, the branches of a weeping elm stretched to the grass, the leaves just starting to change color.

Dickens's mom had put three pots of bright yellow mums on the front steps, along with a decorative straw bale. A wreath of yellow maple leaves hung on the door. All in all, it was as cute as possible. I was just about to say how much I liked the leaf wreath when the front door swung open and Dickens came out calling, "Buster!"

Buster wagged madly and pulled at the leash as Dickens hurried over. They had only met once over the weekend, but they were already best friends. Dickens has that effect on animals; he loves them, and the feeling is always mutual.

"Hi, Dickens." Sheera hitched her backpack higher onto her shoulders. "How's it going?"

Dickens glanced at his house and rolled his eyes. "It's going weirdly," he said, then turned back to Buster. "But I didn't want to miss the chance to say goodbye to this guy before he goes to Hope House! This guy! Yes, this little guy!" Buster had rolled over onto his back and waved his paws in the air with his tongue lolling out of his mouth as Dickens rubbed his belly. "Hey," he said, "make sure the shelter people give his nails a trim; they're getting a little long."

"I wish I had time to bring Buster to Poochalicious for some grooming," I said.

"I'd pay money to see this guy get a dog makeover," Dickens said.

"Oh yeah, for sure," Sheera agreed, and I looked at her in surprise. She hadn't been enthusiastic about the idea when Yasmin brought it up that morning.

"I'll make sure they do it at Hope House," I said. "I'm planning to volunteer there, anyway, so maybe they can teach me to do it."

"Volunteer at the shelter?" Dickens straightened up, folding his arms across his chest.

"Yeah—my aunt says they need people to do some basic stuff, and you only have to be twelve," I explained.

"Oh, awesome, maybe I'll sign up for some hours, too," Dickens said.

"Me, too," Sheera added.

"That's a great idea—after all, you're the one who saved Loretta," Dickens pointed out. Sheera blushed a little, and neither one of them noticed my dubious look. *Saved Loretta?* I thought. *More like ran away screaming every time Loretta appeared.* Which, for some reason, Dickens's pet skink only ever decided to do when Sheera was around. I'd spent days looking for her, but she'd only show up when she had the chance to freak out my friend.

Anyway, I wasn't so sure that Sheera was going to be great with animals, but I thought it was cool that she wanted to volunteer. It would be more fun with all of us.

A moment later, a slender, taller version of Dickens walked out of his house. It was Milton, Dickens's older brother. "Oh, look, it's Dickens's little friends," he said sarcastically.

"Whatever, Milton," I shot back. "I literally remember you eating dirt when you were in second grade, so don't act all cool now."

Sheera bleated a loud *"Ha!"* as Dickens snickered.

Milton scowled in my direction and stormed to the tan Toyota parked in the street. He got in and peeled out, but it didn't really have the effect he was clearly looking for since he had to stop half a block later at a stop sign.

"What was that all about?" I asked.

"Just some drama." Dickens rolled his eyes and shook his head. "Let's all make a pact not to become teenagers."

"My older brother is a teenager, and he's pretty cool," Sheera said.

"Then you're lucky. Listen, I should probably head inside. Glad I caught you two. And you, little buddy. Have a great life—someone's gonna love you!" He gave Buster a final pat and turned to go.

"So this is going to be fun, right?" I said as we headed across the street toward my house. "All of us volunteering! Do you think I should tell Johanna about it? And maybe Yasmin? She likes dogs." I'm subtle, right?

"Maybe Johanna," Sheera said doubtfully.

"Not Yasmin? She has so much experience with dogs!"

Sheera looked tired and heaved a sigh. "I don't know . . . I don't know if I can trust her."

"Maybe she's changed," I suggested. "Like, I had that whole thing with Johanna and Avril last year, remember? And now Johanna and I are friendly again."

"Hunh." Sheera picked up a mottled yellow-and-green maple leaf and twirled it by its stem. "Well, maybe she has changed." She looked up at me and her brown eyes met mine in a level gaze. "But I doubt it."

I didn't want to argue with Sheera, but I wasn't going to give up. "Let's see what happens," I said. "You never know."

CHAPTER THREE

"Thanks so much for bringing us," I said as Zane and I walked up to Hope House, Buster trotting ahead. "I can't believe Mom had to work late again."

"She's been putting in a lot of hours." Zane pulled open one of the glass doors, and Buster and I passed through. "It'll pay off in the long run."

"I know," I said. "But right now, it's a pain. It's lucky you could bring us; otherwise, we wouldn't have made it before closing." I looked down at Buster, who was sniffing around the new space. My heart squeezed a little. He was such a sweet guy; he hadn't been with us long, but I was going to miss him.

"Can I help you?" A plump, gray-haired volunteer with pink cheeks and a name tag that read JODY smiled at us from behind a desk.

"Hi, this is Buster," I said. "And I'm Mackenzie, and we're supposed to be meeting someone named Sarah? For an . . . intake?" Aunt Goldie had told me what to say.

"Sarah's expecting you?" she asked.

"Yes."

The woman looked over at Zane. "I'm with her," he said. "And the dog."

"I'll be right back." Jody flashed us a smile and disappeared down the hall. To our right was a floor-to-ceiling window with a play structure set in front of it. A copper-colored cat was lounging on the top level while two black kittens wrestled below. On the other side of the window, a family stood watching the kittens.

I could see a room beyond with a wall of cages, many of which held cats in various stages of loafing around.

There was also a large structure nearby that held two ferrets, one white and one brown-and-white. I noticed a door with a sign that read SMALL ANIMALS, another with a sign that read DOGS, and another that read BIRDS.

A college-age woman wearing a volunteer button came through the DOGS door, leading a wheezing pug on a leash. The pug came over, and she and Buster sniffed each other, tails wagging. "Come on, Bernice, time for a walk," the volunteer said, and Bernice trotted after her.

"This seems like a really nice place." Zane's head swiveled as he looked around. Then he looked back at me and smiled. "Clean, well run. The animals look happy."

"Yeah." My voice had dried up a little. The shelter did seem nice, but suddenly I was starting to feel nervous. *Would Buster be okay here overnight?* I wondered. *Wouldn't he miss us?* I felt my whole body thump with the thudding of my heart.

Buster sat, his ears pricked.

Jody returned with a youngish, slender woman with dark brown skin and close-cropped hair. "Hi, I'm Sarah. Is this Buster?" she asked with a huge smile.

Hearing his name, Buster stood up and went over to say hello, tail wagging, and Sarah petted and cooed at him.

He'll be fine, I told myself as my ears started to buzz. *He'll be fine he'll be fine he'll be fine—*

Sarah looked up at me. "Has he had his dinner?"

"What? Uh, yes. I fed him before we came over," I told her.

"You're not hungry, then, right, Buster?" Sarah asked. She pulled a treat from her pocket and held it out. Buster sat. "Oh, maybe a little hungry for a treat?" She gave it to him, and he ate it happily.

He'll be fine he'll be fine he'll be—

Sarah gave him a final pat on the side and then stood up. "Okay, so Gwendolyn called and told me all about his health history and faxed the information over this afternoon." Gwendolyn is my Aunt Goldie's name, but nobody in the family calls her that. "So I think we're all set." Sarah held out her hand.

I looked down at the leash I was holding. "Um . . . he'll be okay, right?" I asked as I passed it over.

"We'll take good care of him," she promised, her eyes serious. She seemed like someone who really cared about animals and knew what she was doing. I glanced at Zane, who gave me an encouraging nod.

I looked down at Buster, who was gazing up at me. "He'll probably get adopted pretty fast, right? A cutie like him?"

Sarah smiled and tilted her head a bit. "Well," she said slowly, "it can take some of our seniors a little while to find a home. But he's healthy, so he'll probably find a family in a few weeks."

"A few *weeks*?" I repeated. Somehow, I had imagined that Buster would only have to be in the shelter for a few days. I looked at Zane, who lifted his eyebrows and dropped his lower lip in a *yikes* expression.

"We'll take good care of him," Sarah said again.

Buster gazed at me with huge eyes. Suddenly, I couldn't bear the thought of him staying in the shelter, not even for a night. "Could he keep staying with us?" I asked before I even knew the words were coming. "Temporarily, I mean—while the shelter tries to find him a family?"

Surprise registered on Sarah's face, and she repeated, "You want to foster him?" She looked over at Zane. "What does Dad think?"

Zane pointed to himself. "Who, me?"

"Oh, that's not my dad," I told her. "He's my mom's kind-of-sort-of boyfriend."

Zane shook his head as Sarah pursed her lips. "I'm just the chauffeur today," he explained.

"I already signed up online to volunteer here," I said.

Then I added, "And I talked my friends into doing it, too," just to seem like a good citizen.

"So, here's the thing about fostering." Sarah folded her arms across her chest and leaned against the wall. "You have to go through a training session and fill out some paperwork. You could do the training online, but you'll need a parent to sign for you."

"What about Aunt Goldie?" I suggested. "Gwendolyn Marks, my aunt? Maybe she could sign for me?"

"What about your parents?"

"Mom's at work and my dad lives in Denver. But I know my mom would say yes."

Sarah seemed to think it over.

"Could you at least call my aunt?" I begged.

Sarah huffed a little chuckle, then looked down at Buster. "Are you a lucky dog?" she asked him, and he wagged. "Give me a minute," Sarah said, and she pulled a phone out of her pocket and headed toward her office.

"We should call your mom," Zane suggested.

"She's in a client meeting," I pointed out. "I'm sure that she'll be fine with fostering Buster a little while longer—she already said that she wished he could stay with us a few more days. Besides, we can always bring him here if we need to—right?"

I glanced over at Jody, who was still standing nearby. "Absolutely," she agreed.

"Okay," Sarah said as she walked back toward us. "Gwendolyn has said that she'll take full responsibility and that Buster will do well in your home, so I'm going to allow this. I'll go get the paperwork."

"Yay, Bustie!" I said, giving him a pat. He danced a little, hopping left and right. He could tell there was some reason to be excited and probably hoped it would involve more treats.

I heard clicking toenails and a wheeze and looked up to see the elderly pug and her walker were back. "You guys are still here?" the volunteer asked.

"We're going to foster Buster," I said.

"Oh, that's great! Well, maybe I'll see you all at Pet-A-Palooza," she said.

"What's that?"

Jody pulled a flyer out of the desk drawer and handed it to me. "It's a big adoption event we do every year," she explained. "I heard you say that you're going to volunteer. This is a great event to help out with."

"Perfect!" I looked up at Zane.

"Don't look at me," he said with a little smile. "Just the chauffeur, remember?"

"You're already helping plenty," I told him. I smiled down at the papers. This would be so fun! I couldn't wait to tell my mom all about Buster and volunteering at the shelter once I got home. I knew she'd be as excited as I was.

Mom was not as excited as I was.

"Why is that dog back here?" she asked from her place on the couch. She was still wearing her work clothes—nice navy slacks and a button-down pink shirt—but she had untucked the shirt and kicked off her shoes. Her eyeliner was a little smeary on the left eye and she looked like what she was—tired.

"Yay! Bustie gets to stay with us a little longer!" I said, trying to "pep talk" her into getting excited. I made two little fists and gave them a half-hearted pump. "Uh . . . yaaay?"

Buster was completely oblivious to this chat and hopped up onto the couch to step on my mom's stomach and lick her cheek. "What are you doing here, hunh?" she asked him, rubbing his side. Her voice was gentler and she shook her head as she gave Zane the side-eye. "Please tell me that you two did not adopt this dog. Because I haven't even eaten dinner yet."

"It smells great in here, by the way," I said quickly.

"That's pizza. It's on the table; we can eat in a minute. Now tell me you didn't adopt Buster."

"No! Of course not, no." Zane's eyes were huge, and I think he was worried that he was about to be demoted from kind-of-sort-of boyfriend to out-in-the-garbage status.

"We're going to foster him," I said. "Just for a week or two. I thought it would be okay with you, Mom. I'm so sorry."

"I can't believe the shelter didn't even call your parents!"

"Uh, they called Aunt Goldie," I admitted.

Mom's eyes narrowed. "That sister of mine," she grumbled. Turning to Zane, she added, "And why didn't *you* stop this?"

He blinked in surprise and said, *"Yo no hablo ingles."*

Mom laughed and tossed a throw pillow at Zane, who ducked. "Oh, you don't speak English now?"

"I'm an immigrant," he protested. "I didn't understand what was happening!"

Mom rolled her eyes. "You're so full of it. You came to this country when you were ten; you're a bestselling author, for heaven's sake! You aren't even from a Spanish-speaking country—why didn't you say that you can't speak English in Urdu?"

"I thought you might not know what I was saying," Zane admitted. "Because you don't speak any Urdu."

"Good thinking," I told him. "Then you would have had to explain it in English."

"Exactly." Zane nodded. "Thanks."

Mom leaned back against the couch pillow and Buster flopped halfway across her lap. "This dog is ruining my good work pants," she complained as she stroked his fur.

"I can brush them off," I volunteered.

Mom waved her hand. "It's fine; I have a lint roller." She gazed at Buster as Zane widened his eyes at me in an *I can't believe you got me into trouble* glare.

Mom heaved a sigh and looked up at me. "Mackenzie, how is this going to work? I'm out of the house all day. Dogs need attention. Who's going to walk him?"

"I'll walk him," I promised.

"What about your after-school activities?" Mom demanded.

I had been going to something called finishing school on Wednesdays, which was really more of an art club. "I'll tell Alyce that I can't make it for a couple of weeks. And on Thursdays, I'll just bring Bustie with me when I head over to Poppy's."

"And Buster can stay with me in the mornings," Zane offered. He works from his home office.

I was just about to say "No, I've got it"—but then I remembered that I'm supposed to accept help sometimes. "That—that would be great, Zane. Thanks."

Zane shoved his hands into his pockets. "I mean, this is partially my fault," he admitted.

"Partially?" Mom prompted.

"*Que?*" Zane asked, using Spanish again, and Mom shook her head. "But Mackenzie, you'll have to show me what to do," he added. "I'm not a pet guy, remember? I don't know what I'm doing here."

"No problem!" I patted Mom's shoulder. "Mom, it's going to be okay. You won't even notice he's here."

"Mackenzie, dogs get sick and have to go to the vet.

They have accidents on the floor. They need to be played with and trained." Buster seemed to know that she was getting upset. He placed a paw over her heart. "No offense, friend," she told him. "I just . . . I like Buster, but we really don't have the bandwidth to adopt him."

"I know, Mom. This is temporary, I swear. I just . . . I couldn't leave him there. If he's going to someone's home, I'll feel okay, but—" I was getting a little teary.

"It's fine," Mom said. "I understand. Really. I just want to make sure that you know that he can't be our dog. I can only do this for a little while."

"How long?"

"Two weeks."

"Two weeks," I repeated. "No problem. I'll get Bustie a home in two weeks, easy!"

Mom looked down at Buster and cupped her hands around his face. "Troublemaker," she said, rubbing his ears with her thumbs. He closed his eyes happily. "Okay." Mom gently shifted him to the side so that she could stand up. "Let's all wash our hands and have some pizza."

"Yay, little buddy!" I said as Buster hopped off the couch. "You're rolling with us!"

"For two weeks," Mom repeated.

I put my hand over my heart. "Promise."

"*No problemo*," Zane added, and Mom threw another pillow at him.

Which I took as a good sign. For all of us.

DIY: How to Make Things Stick

That was close. I nearly messed things up there with Zane, which would be a disaster.

My mom doesn't like to date. And now that she's so busy at her job, she doesn't have much time to go out. I'd spent a good amount of time trying to get her a boyfriend, and I'd failed. Hard.

Zane was just a lucky break—a nice guy who happened to live next door. Perfect!

But also kind of scary. Because my mom dating Zane was a bit of a high-wire act. No net. I mean, the guy lives next door! What if they *break up*?

We'd still have to say hi to him every day, and my mom would probably never meet anyone else, and the whole thing would be hideously awkward. We'd just have to wait for him to move out so that maybe some nice new guy could move in and my mom could meet another human being. But given that Zane had lived in his apartment for ten years already, I didn't think we had that kind of time.

Luckily, my gamble paid off, and my mom really was okay with Buster staying a little longer. And she hadn't blamed Zane. But I couldn't let them break up, especially not over something that I did.

I had to be more careful.

CHAPTER FOUR

There is a funky little café about two blocks from my house called the Pie Salon, and it's made to look like a 1950s beauty parlor. That sounds weird, but it's cute—they have these old-fashioned pink hair-dryer-helmet chairs, and you can sit there and eat a slice of pie and all the servers will call you "hon" and smack their gum. The walls are covered in black-and-white posters of 1950s movie stars like Marilyn Monroe, Eartha Kitt, and Audrey Hepburn. It's a whole thing.

They specialize in pie, and not just sweet kinds, either. They have spicy meat hand pies and quiche, too. Not that you'd eat quiche in a 1950s hair salon. Come to think of it, you probably wouldn't eat any kind of pie in any kind of hair salon. But I'm getting off the topic.

It was Wednesday, and when I told Sheera and Johanna that I had to skip finishing school, they offered to take care of Buster with me. We threw the ball for him in the backyard for a while, and then Johanna got the idea to see what he would do if we blew bubbles. Bustie was super into that, chasing them around and popping them with his nose.

"I'm hungry," Sheera said after a while.

Oh, and the best thing about the Pie Salon? They have a walk-up window for people who are in a state of piemergency.

We took Buster with us. After a bit of discussion, we agreed to get two slices of pie—Key lime and strawberry rhubarb—and three forks. Johanna and I got iced tea, and Sheera got an orange seltzer. Just as we finished placing our orders at the window, a group of girls our age spilled out the front door of the restaurant. "Oh, ugh," Sheera muttered.

"What's up?" Johanna asked as we made our way to one of the umbrella tables.

"Yasmin's friends," Sheera said. "From Greenwood Academy."

One of the girls noticed us, then whispered to her blonde friend. The blonde looked over and gave Sheera this scrunchy-faced smile and waved.

Sheera cocked her head and waved back, but didn't smile.

"So you know them?" I asked.

"It's pretty rare for them to remember who I am or to acknowledge my presence," Sheera said. "But yes. I've met them like five hundred times."

"I still can't believe Yasmin managed to get on the front page of the school paper with that cute dog T-shirt," Johanna said. "One day in school and everyone already knows her."

Sheera glowered. "Speak of the devil," she said.

"Hey! Look who's here!" cried a voice behind me, and when I looked over, I saw Yasmin and a glamorous woman walking toward us. Yasmin's mother was wearing black boots, black pants, and a black tunic with a cropped denim jacket. Several long gold necklaces hung from her neck, and black hair flowed down her back. Her nails were done, her eyebrows were done, her makeup was perfect, and her sunglasses looked like they were roughly as expensive as my mom's car . . . in other words, she was about five sizes too fashionable for our small town.

When I had pictured Yasmin's mom, I had expected someone covered in dog fur, and instead I got someone covered in fabulous.

"What kind of pie did you guys get? Green? What is that, lime?" Yasmin asked as she came over. "Oh, Johanna and Mackenzie, this is my mom. And Mom, this is Buster—I told you about him."

"You can call me Leila," Yasmin's mom said. "Hi, girls. Hi, Sheera! And hi, Buster." He was lying in the shade under my chair, and she bent down to pat him.

"Nice to meet you," I told her. "Are you here for some pie?"

"We're doing a little birthday thing for one of our groomers," Leila said. "She likes pie better than cake, so I'm picking one up. I'll be right back." She walked over to the pickup window.

"Yasmin, Rachel and those guys are here." Sheera jerked her head in the direction of the girls who were standing near the corner, probably waiting to be picked up.

The blonde one—Rachel, I guess—lifted her hand, and Yasmin waved back. But she didn't go over to say hi. Instead, she turned back to me. "So, Mackenzie, since Buster is staying with you a little longer, you should definitely bring him to Poochalicious for a makeover!" She knelt down to scratch behind his ears, but he had found a piece of piecrust on the ground and was distracted. "We'll give this cutie the works. And maybe we can find some new toys for him, too."

"We were just playing around with some bubbles," Johanna volunteered. "Buster loved it."

"You should get one of those baby pools," Yasmin suggested. "Just fill it with water; some dogs love to splash."

"Okay, I've got the pie." Leila reappeared, holding a large white bakery box. "I hope she likes cherry."

"I've had it; it's delicious," I said.

"Oh, good!" Leila swept her hair over her shoulder. "I couldn't decide, so I told them to surprise me."

"Bye!" Yasmin said as she and her mom headed toward their white car. Yasmin turned and waved as she walked.

Sheera watched her, a dark expression on her face. "That was weird."

"Running into them at the Pie Salon?" Johanna asked, scooping up the last forkful of strawberry rhubarb. "Or getting a pie instead of a birthday cake?"

"Neither—I mean the fact that Yasmin didn't say anything to Rachel." Sheera looked toward where the girls had been standing, but they must have gotten picked up while I wasn't watching. "She didn't even shout hello."

"It seemed like her mom was in a hurry," I said.

"More like Yasmin didn't want to talk to them." Sheera shrugged. "That's how she is—she blows people off."

"Hm." I wasn't sure how to reply. It seemed just as likely that Yasmin's friends were being cold to *her*. After all, they didn't come over and say hi, either.

"Something's up." Sheera had already drained her seltzer. She sipped a piece of ice and crunched it. "I know my cousin better than she knows herself."

"Or we'll see that this is not a big deal and you're reading way too much into this," I said.

"I know I'm right," Sheera said.

"But maybe you're wrong," I told her.

We both looked at Johanna. "I'm not a part of this," she announced.

Sheera turned back to me and gestured with her fork. "I'm going to find out what's up and why Yasmin left Greenwood," Sheera said. "You'll see."

"*Someone* will see *something*," I said, trying to make my voice sound ominous.

Johanna looked from me to Sheera, then back again. "Yes, I think we can all agree that someone's going to see something." She looked at her phone. "I have to get home, though, so let's head out, okay?"

Sheera is so stubborn! I thought as we bused our dishes. *She always wants to be right.*

But I could be stubborn, too, and I wasn't going to give up until she and her cousin were friends again. My plate clattered into the gray bin, setting the forks rattling.

We were all going to get along, and I was going to make it happen, and Sheera would see that I was right, and that would be that.

"Hey!" Zane called as we headed up the front walk. "Where've you two been?"

"The Pie Salon," I told him. "Then we walked Johanna to her house."

"Well, I have a surprise for you!" He darted into his side of the duplex and came out brandishing something with a tag on it. "For a very special someone."

"Where'd you get the dog bone?" Sheera asked.

"This, my dear niece, is not a bone. It's an antler. Deer shed them naturally and—apparently—they're great for dogs to chew on because unlike bones, they don't splinter." Zane looked very proud of himself.

"I thought you weren't a pet guy," I teased as Zane pulled the tag off the antler and handed it to me.

"There's something called the internet," Zane replied. "Lots of good information there; you should check it out. I've also got a sister-in-law who knows a lot about dogs, so . . ."

Behind me, gravel crunched as my mom pulled into the driveway. "Excellent timing," I said.

"Hey, everyone!" Mom called as she got out of the car.

"You're in a good mood," I said as Mom pulled her leather tote bag out of the backseat and slung it over her shoulder.

"I didn't have to stay late, for once," she replied. "Good to see you, Sheera! Have you all been taking Buster for a walk?" She knelt down to rub his ears. "That's nice of you to help out," Mom said to Sheera.

"It's no problem; I like Buster," Sheera said. "He's much better than that lizard that used to hide in your cabinets."

Everyone laughed, knowing she meant Dickens's pet blue-tongued skink, Loretta.

"I've got to get going," Sheera said. "See you tomorrow, Kenzie."

"Oh, Sheera, before you leave, why don't you and your family come over some weekend?" Mom suggested. "We can have a barbecue. Lunch on Saturday?"

I let out an excited squeak. Mom had remembered my barbecue idea! *Thanks, Buster,* I thought. *Because of you, Mom is relaxed enough to consider it.*

"Sounds fun." Sheera lifted her eyebrows at me and I nodded encouragingly. "I'll have to check with my parents."

"Just let Mackenzie know what they say," Mom said.

"Okay." Sheera nodded and took off.

Mom was still waving enthusiastically when she noticed that Zane and I were looking at her. "What?" she asked.

"Thanks, Mom!" I said, giving her a hug. "This is so sweet of you since I know how much you hate to cook."

"Mackenzie!" Mom looked outraged. "I cook almost every night!"

"Yes, but don't you complain about it?"

She pursed her lips. "Well . . . I'll just make . . ." Her eyes widened and she looked over at Zane.

"Yes?" Zane prompted.

"What should I make?" Mom asked. "What does your brother and his family like?"

He smiled. "They're pretty easy to please," he said. "But . . ."

"What?" Mom looked nervous.

"Well, they only eat halal. Usually. I mean, technically they won't have to if they're eating here, but—"

"I can make something halal," Mom said quickly. "Um . . . do you know where I can get something halal?"

Zane laughed. "I can take you to the butcher, or you can buy kosher meat at the supermarket."

"Wait—kosher and halal are the same?" I asked.

"No, not the same, but very similar," Zane explained. "Kosher meat would work for them. And I'll help with everything . . . I am invited, right?"

"No," Mom told him. "You are not invited. Your attendance is *mandatory*."

"Really, don't get too worried," Zane assured her. "My brother Rizwan is pretty easygoing. I don't think he and Veena will expect you to do anything fancy."

"And I'll help you plan," I promised. "But you do know that Sheera has brothers, right?"

"What? How many?"

"Just two. One older, one much younger, like four or five."

Mom mashed her lips together, clearly realizing that this was a slightly bigger project than she had anticipated. "Well, it's just a barbecue! The more the merrier, right?" She smiled and we all headed to our front doors.

"Okay, I'll see you guys later," Zane said. "Maybe I can make dinner for all of us over here tomorrow, since I'll be enjoying barbecue in a couple of weeks."

"Sounds great!" Mom gave him a little toodle-oo wave. Once we were inside, she closed the door and leaned against it.

"Mom, thanks so much for doing this. I'm sure you're really going to like Sheera's family." I know a barbecue is no big deal, but my mom had been really busy lately and she is also not really crazy about parties or going out in general. She likes reading, making quilts, or watching the Hallmark Channel.

Mom dropped her tote by the door and placed her keys

on the hook. "Oh, this is going to be fine. I've got every-thing under control, right?" Toenails scrabbled against the wood floor and Buster hurried to greet us—

—with a trash can on his head. It was the narrow one that usually sat beside the toilet.

"Oh my—" Mom dashed over to rescue him as I traced the pile of discarded tissues and Q-tips back to the bath-room. I hurried to the kitchen to dig a plastic bag out of the bunch we keep under the sink. I started collecting gross bathroom trash as Mom held on to Buster with one arm and FaceTimed Goldie with the other.

"Hey, what's up?" I heard Goldie say. "I'm actually at the grocery store—"

Mom cut her off. "Buster got into the trash."

My aunt's voice turned serious. "Did he eat anything?"

"I don't know," Mom admitted. Buster growled and squirmed, and Mom tightened her grip on him. "Stop that."

"It was the bathroom trash!" I called. A cold numbness spread across my chest and I felt sick to my stomach, and it wasn't just because of the gross mucus-infected Kleenex in my hand. I hurried to the phone and added, "I threw away some makeup samples and junk like that. Q-tips. And these gross old hair clips—I don't really know if everything's here or not." I dug around in the plastic bag—I really couldn't tell if anything I'd thrown away was missing. I mean, who remembers what you throw away? The whole point is to forget about it, right?

"You should probably get him X-rayed," Goldie said. "Because that stuff can get lodged in his intestine and cause real problems. Listen, I can buy this hummus later. I'll meet you guys at the clinic in ten minutes, okay?"

Mom nodded, and Goldie's face disappeared from the screen. "We've got to go."

"Naughty dog," I told Buster, but he just looked at me with a silly dog grin, like he was really proud of himself. "Should I stay here and make dinner so it's ready when you come home?" I asked Mom.

"I want you to hold on to Buster while I drive," Mom said. "We'll worry about food later. Maybe we should have let Goldie get that hummus." Mom grabbed her keys with the hand that wasn't holding Buster, and I grabbed her purse as we ran out the door.

It was kind of amazing how quickly things could go from totally under control to totally a huge disaster.

Cost of animal hospital emergency room visit: $80.

Cost of dog X-ray with a Friends-and-Family discount: $150.

Cost of takeout because we were too exhausted to cook and Goldie didn't have her hummus: $53.

Having a bad old foster dog who actually didn't swallow a hair clip but is now obsessed with tissues: Well, I wanna say priceless, but actually $283 total, plus a ruined evening, plus now my homework's gonna be late and Mom has to stay up until midnight to finish her report. And she's stressed out instead of relaxed.

So, yeah, priceless. But not exactly free.

It was Saturday morning, and I was back at the animal shelter. Sheera and Dickens had come along, and Aunt Goldie was giving us a tour of the facility. Buster was used to spending the mornings next door, so Zane said he could hang out with him while I was gone.

"Here's where the rabbits live," Aunt Goldie said as she

pulled open the door to the Small Animal area. There were four large enclosures, three of which held rabbit pairs. A big floppy-eared, fawn-colored bunny sat in the fourth cage. "This is Peanut Butter," my aunt said when I approached. "She's really friendly and mellow."

"I love the muff at her neck," I said.

"I know. She's a Holland Lop; that's standard for the breed."

"They're kind of messy." Sheera frowned at the hay scattered across the floor.

"I can relate," Dickens said. "This looks like my room."

Aunt Goldie introduced us to a couple of chinchillas, which were the softest things I'd ever felt. Dickens and I got to hold the white ferret, Snowball, and then we went to visit the birds.

"Who's this?" Sheera asked as Goldie opened a cockatiel's cage.

"This is Albert," my aunt said. "Want to hold him?"

Sheera is usually a little skittish around animals, but Goldie showed her how to hold out her finger, and Albert hopped on. "I love his dinosaur feet," Sheera said, bringing Albert up to eye level and peering at his bumpy pinkish-gray skin and long gray claws. Albert leaned forward and reached under her red headscarf with his beak to pull out a tendril of black hair. "Hey!"

"He's preening you," Goldie explained.

"I get it, I need to wash my hair," Sheera said as she pulled him away.

"No—it means he likes you," Dickens said, which made Sheera blush.

"Oh. I guess I don't know how to tell when a bird is into me." She laughed uncomfortably, and Albert cocked his head, shrugging his wings. "Okay, okay, we can be friends." Goldie took Albert from Sheera's finger and placed him in his cage as Sheera tucked her hair back under her scarf.

"Cats next," Goldie announced.

There were five kittens in different enclosures—one fluffy tabby, a calico, two black cats, and a tiny gray cutie with blue eyes. An older woman with white hair wrapped across the top of her head in braids watched the older cats climbing and lounging on the structure.

"Hi, Greta," my aunt said to the older woman. "How's Penny today?"

"Oh, she's just fine," Greta said, smiling at a large copper tabby. "She's lounging near the window, as usual." Penny was draped across the length of a carpet-lined windowsill, her tail hanging down and twitching slightly.

"Are you adopting her?" I asked.

Greta shook her head, still watching the cat. "No, dear, I just like to come in and visit," she said. "Penny reminds me of a cat I had when I was a girl. His name was Charlie."

"Well, maybe it's time for another cat," I said brightly.

Greta laughed a little. "I don't think so." Then she smiled at us apologetically, cast a last glance at Penny, and walked out.

Aunt Goldie watched her go. "She's here every Saturday," she said. "Sometimes more often. She wants that cat."

"Then why doesn't she take Penny home?" Sheera asked. "What's stopping her?"

Goldie shrugged and said, "Who knows? But one thing I've learned from volunteering here—you can't push people. They're not ready until they're ready."

We made our way through the dog section and into the yard, where two elderly cocker spaniels were playing tug-of-war with a rope toy. It was so adorable that I snapped a photo on my phone.

"Cute," Dickens said when I held it up.

When I showed it to Aunt Goldie, she said, "Oh, send that to me, would you? Sometimes we put extra pictures and videos up on the website, along with the animal's profile. That can really help get them adopted."

"Maybe I should take more photos of Buster," I said.

"Or some video," Dickens suggested.

"Great idea." Goldie nodded, then turned back to me. "Do you know how to edit them together?"

"I could probably figure it out," I told her. "I'll just google how to do it."

"Okay, but let me know if you need help," Goldie replied.

Oh, right: *Ask for help if I need it*. I made a mental note to remember, and that if I couldn't figure things out after two hours, I'd call my aunt. Maybe three hours. Anyway, I'd probably be able to figure it out.

We walked back through the main dog area, where classical music was playing and the dogs were chilling. One sweet-faced brindle pit bull stood up to wag when he saw Goldie.

"Oscar!" she called softly. "How's my sweet little guy, hunh?"

She opened the cage, and when she went inside, Oscar rolled over onto his back, demanding a belly rub. "So ferocious," Goldie teased as she knelt down beside him. "What a big, strong, scary pit bull, right? Right, sweetie?" Oscar's tail swished back and forth in agreement. Aunt Goldie looked up at me. "His former owners said he was aggressive," she said as Oscar wriggled in delight. "Does this guy look aggressive to you?"

"About as aggressive as a jelly doughnut," Sheera said. Dickens laughed.

"Yeah, and as terrifying," Dickens agreed. He smiled at her and she chuckled.

I felt like I had to add something, so I said, "And as dangerous."

Nobody laughed.

"Exactly," Aunt Goldie said after a beat. "He's a big marshmallow." She shook her head and sighed. "Sometimes it's the circumstances that make them aggressive. Still, he'll need a special home. Once they're labeled aggressive, you have to be careful where you place them. We wouldn't want him to go into a home with a small child, just in case something bad happens."

Oscar closed his eyes slowly, enjoying the attention.

"But doesn't that cut down on the number of people who can adopt him?" I asked.

"Yep. He's been here three months already." Goldie stroked his forehead and he wiggled happily. "Poor guy."

She must have noticed that my eyes were filling with tears because she added, "Don't worry, Kenz. We'll find him the right home."

"He's just such a good dog," Dickens murmured.

Goldie gave Oscar a final pat and stood up. "They're all good dogs. And we're going to find every single one of them a good family—the family they deserve."

I nodded. "You're right; we will."

Goldie blinked. "I actually meant 'we,' as in the shelter."

"Well, I'm talking about 'we,' as in me," I told her. "All these guys—the ferrets, the birds, the kittens—we're getting this done!" I smacked my fist into my palm.

"Here she goes," Dickens said.

Sheera laughed, which annoyed me. Yes, I was going to help! I didn't think that was so crazy.

Aunt Goldie smiled. "Love it," she said, leading me back into the front entranceway and pointing toward the front desk, where I was supposed to spend the next hour greeting people. "Start by giving everyone a smile when they come in. I'm heading back to the vet station. Let me know if you need help."

"I will," I told her. But I didn't need help.

I just needed a *plan*.

CHAPTER FIVE

It was lucky that I had the rest of the weekend because it took me a few hours to get the video of Buster just the way I wanted it. First, I took some footage of him begging, then some of him chasing a ball (I cut the part where I had to run after him to get the ball back), then some of him snuggling against my legs with his paws in the air, being cute. Then I added some upbeat music and some title text saying, MEET BUSTER! HE'S A VERY GOOD BOY! and all his information— nine years old, Jack Russell, active, etc. I tried to sync it up so that his tail was wagging on the beat.

Then I decided that I should show people how smart he was, so I made a puzzle out of some dog treats, tennis balls, and a muffin tin. I just put a few treats in the muffin cups, then covered the treats with tennis balls. The first time, Buster got so excited that he stepped on the muffin tin and it flipped up, sending balls bouncing everywhere and treats flying. But the next time I did it, Buster looked very cute nosing the balls out of the way to get to the treats, so that's the part that went into the video.

I briefly considered doing a blooper reel but decided against it.

The finished video was only two minutes long but it took *forever*, mostly because I didn't know how to use the video tools. But NOW I know and I love it!

I sent the video to Aunt Goldie, and I also sent it to Sheera, Dickens, and Johanna. I sent it to Yasmin, too, since she had given me her phone number. Actually, she was the one who was the most excited about it.

I also sent it to my mom and my grandfather, and to my dad.

Dad lives in Denver—he got remarried at the beginning of this year and has a stepson about my age, Emilio. Wow, it's really weird to say that my dad has a stepson. Not that it's weird for someone to have a stepson. It's only weird for *my dad* to have a stepson. Which means that I have a stepbrother. Honestly, though, I don't really think about Emilio much.

I'm going to just say it: Emilio is kind of annoying.

Anyway, Dad and I usually chat on Monday nights, but when he got the video, my phone rang right away.

"Hey!" Dad said. "Great video! Who's the dog? What's the story with that?"

"Oh—that's Buster. Mom and I are just fostering him for a little while until he finds a home. Isn't he cute?" Buster was right beside me on the couch, so I scritched his ear, which made his leg twitch as if he were running.

"Well . . . he seems a little *old*," Dad said.

The top of my chest tightened and I felt a flush at the bottom of my neck. "He isn't old," I snapped. "He's only nine."

I heard someone say something to Dad and him replying, "Okay, just give me five." Then he said to me, "That's very old for a dog. I mean, I remember with Harpo—older dogs can be a lot of work."

"Buster is very healthy!"

"*Now* he's healthy. But he'll get older, and . . ." My dad scoffed a little, and I swear that I wanted to reach through the phone and throttle him. *My dad and Emilio are* both *annoying,* I thought, rolling my eyes.

Buster wasn't old the way that a ninety-year-old is old. He was old the way a fifty-year-old who works out is old: some gray, but still in shape.

And anyone who adopted Buster would be lucky to have him!

"Dad, Buster is a great dog. He's totally cuddly and cute and happy and playful. He's great on a leash. He's good with other dogs; he just hates squirrels, and—"

"All right, all right, don't take it personally. I'm not saying anything against Buster. I'm just saying that some people might not want to get an older dog." There was a short pause, then I heard him murmur, "Yep, coming. I'll be right there."

"Are you at work? It's Sunday night!"

I heard the sound of papers shuffling. "Unfortunately. Big meeting tomorrow with some potential partners." My dad owns a potato factory that produces frozen mashed potatoes: Potasteez. "It's only three o'clock here; I'll be home for dinner."

I did not point out that on Sunday, you're supposed to be home *all day*. But that's my dad—he really likes to work.

"Look, Dad, I don't need a hundred people to adopt Buster," I pointed out. "I only need one."

He chuckled. "Fair point. To tell you the truth, Emilio has been talking about getting a dog lately, too. But I don't know. It's so much work . . ."

"It's also fun, though," I said. "You always said that anything worth doing is hard work, right? You should get one! And I know a good dog who is already housebroken . . ."

Dad laughed. "I don't think we'll be flying Buster out to Denver anytime soon. Okay, listen, I've got to go. We'll chat again tomorrow, okay?"

"Sounds good." I touched my phone screen and Dad's name disappeared. "Can you believe that guy?" I asked Buster. "Saying you're too old." Buster tilted his head and wagged uncertainly. I loved it when he tried to figure out what I was saying. I patted him on the head. "Let's watch the video again," I said. And Buster, being a very sweet boy, didn't argue.

"Where did Buster get that cute raincoat?" Sheera asked. It was the next day, and we were walking Buster through the park again after school. This had become our new routine—leave school together, grab a purple energy drink

(Sheera's favorite) from the store nearby, drop off our backpacks at my house, pick up Buster from Zane's, and take him for a stroll.

A light drizzle—almost a mist—fell from the film of gray clouds overhead, but it didn't seem like it really wanted to rain. It was more like the sky was in a bad mood and not up to being all bright and sunny *or* all stormy. The fallen leaves were damp and kept sticking to our shoes, but it was only a little cold. I could smell the faint, sweet-smoky scent of someone in the neighborhood using their fireplace.

"The raincoat?" I repeated, wishing a little that she hadn't noticed. "Uh, well. Yasmin, actually. She made it for Buster. Isn't that amazing?" At the sound of his name, Buster turned back, trotted up to me, and sat expectantly. "You're a handsome boy, aren't you, buddy?" I petted his ears; his fur was clammy from the chill mist.

We fell into step again, walking toward my street. "I wonder what she did," Sheera said after a moment.

"I think she just used a sewing machine?"

Sheera looked at me sideways. "Not that," she replied. "I wonder what she did to get kicked out of Greenwood Academy."

"Sheera!" I shook my head. "She didn't get kicked out."

"Why else would she leave halfway through the first semester?" Sheera demanded. "I keep asking and nobody in the family is talking about it. Which means it must be something *bad*."

A breeze sent a chill across my neck. I shivered. "Sheera, you're just guessing." I didn't want to argue about it, but the truth was that Yasmin seemed friendly and nice. I liked her style, her nails, how much she liked dogs, how friendly she was. Sure, she was different from Sheera, but that was okay. "I know you guys weren't getting along last year—"

"We used to be like sisters," Sheera blurted. "And then she got those new friends and stopped talking to me." Her eyes were like a storm.

"But that happened to me, too, remember? With Johanna?" I put a hand on Sheera's sleeve. "And we worked it out."

"That's different," Sheera insisted.

"How?"

"Because that isn't *Yasmin*!"

That made me laugh, and I gave Sheera a playful shove. "You're so stubborn!"

Her mouth twisted into a smile. "It's my best quality," she insisted. "No, but really—"

"Hey, Goosie! Hey, Sheera!" Turning, we saw Dickens running up behind us. He was wearing a tank top, shorts, and running shoes despite the cold. "And Buster! Looking good in that coat!"

Buster went wild, wiggling all over the place and jumping up on Dickens's legs as he crouched down to pet him. Buster hopped onto his hind legs to give Dickens a lick. I swear, there is not an animal alive that doesn't love Dickens.

"Cross-country practice?" I asked.

"Last practice of the season," Dickens replied between licks. "Uchh—pfft!" Buster had managed to lick his face while Dickens was talking. "Stop that, buddy." Gently, Dickens grabbed Buster's two front paws, then frowned. "This guy still hasn't gotten his nails done."

"I'm going to take him to the self-grooming station at Poochalicious," I said.

"Hey, can I come?" Dickens asked. "I'd like to see that place."

"Yeah, and I can come and help out, too," Sheera

volunteered. I must have looked pretty surprised because she added, "You know, since my aunt owns it, I know it pretty well."

"I think . . . I mean, I think Yasmin was going to show me around," I said carefully. I wanted Sheera to know that—you know—Yasmin would be there, in case she wanted to bail.

"Then I'll *definitely* come," Sheera said sweetly. She glanced at Dickens and smiled. "Yasmin is my cousin," she explained, and he nodded. I was about to ask her why she was being so nice about Yasmin all of a sudden, but Dickens cut me off.

"That's cool," he said. Then he turned back to me. "When are you taking him?"

"Well, I can't do it tonight—"

"No, me, neither," Dickens agreed.

"Okay, so—tomorrow?" Dickens and Sheera both nodded, so I added, "I'll check in with my mom, but it'll have to be after work, like five thirty? I'll text you if she says no."

"Just meet at your house?" Dickens asked.

"Yeah."

Sheera smiled, then pressed her lips together and looked

around nonchalantly, like she was really interested in a nearby oak tree.

"Sounds great!" Dickens said, straightening up. "Listen, I need to finish this run. I'll see you guys later!" He veered off toward the lake to take the loop back to the school track.

"Hm," Sheera said, smiling a little to herself. "This will be fun. Going to Poochalicious, I mean."

"It will?"

Sheera smiled even wider. "Of course."

What the heck?

And then it dawned on me—she was taking my advice! She was going to try to make up with Yasmin, just as I'd suggested!

Wow, she's less stubborn than I thought, I realized.

And I'm even more of a genius.

CHAPTER SIX

Poochalicious took up a good chunk of the strip mall across the bridge. It was located along with two other small shops between the Whole Foods and the Target, which seemed like a pretty decent location, like maybe people dropped off their dogs while they went shopping for groceries and home decor.

The minute we walked in, the guy behind the counter, who looked like he spent most days modeling for upscale brands, smiled and said, "Hi! Are you here for the six p.m. Puppy Yoga class?"

Dickens and I looked at each other and lifted our eyebrows while my mom laughed.

"I wish!" I said.

Dickens narrowed his eyes. "Can we watch that?"

Counter Guy—whose name tag read MATT—laughed.

"I'm afraid that the class is only open to those with a reservation."

"We're here to give this guy a bath," Sheera announced, pointing to Buster, who was tugging at the leash to get to the dog snack display.

"What a cute little guy!" Matt tapped at the tablet computer. "Does he have a reservation at the spa, or are you here to use the self-wash?"

Mom was reading the chalkboard that featured their spa offerings—everything from nail trims to grooming that included the "scent of the month"—and noted, "This place is more expensive than where *I* get my hair cut."

Matt grinned, showing off his even white teeth. "Well, I'll bet most of the customers there don't bite."

"Most of them," Mom admitted.

A doorway behind Matt opened and Yasmin appeared. "Mackenzie! Oh, and Sheera's here!" She looked over her shoulder. "Mom! They're here!"

Leila appeared, this time wearing a white scoop-neck T-shirt with POOCHALICIOUS on the front and black yoga pants. Somehow she still managed to look totally glamorous. "Sheera! So good to see you!" She gave Sheera a kiss on the cheek, then turned to my mom. "Hi! I'm Leila."

"I'm Allison. And this is my daughter, Mackenzie, and her friend Dickens." The tiny lines at the corner of my mom's eyes crinkled as she shook Leila's hand.

"Yes, I've met Mackenzie. Nice to meet you, Dickens."

"Hey, Dickens!" Yasmin said. "You're in my social studies class, I think?"

He nodded and gestured around. "This is such a cool place!"

Leila's laugh was open and genuine. "Some people think it's silly, but we have a lot of fun. Fun is an undervalued resource; it's where we make some of our strongest connections with others, and with our animals."

A tiny puffball of a Pomeranian trotted out of the office and stood at Leila's ankles. "This is Bear."

Bear hopped over to Buster and bowed deeply, a dog signal that she wanted to play. Buster ignored her and kept staring longingly at the treats.

"Mom, I told these guys that they could use the self-wash," Yasmin said.

"Of course! Matty, please get my friends all set up with

some shampoo and towels. And there's no charge for the service," she added.

Mom was already reaching into her purse. "Oh, no, I insist!"

"Don't be silly!" Leila insisted. "I hear our little friend is a foster! We have to do all we can to make sure he looks his best so he can find his forever home. Now, if you'll excuse me, I have to lead a yoga class."

"I'm the assistant," Yasmin said. "So we'll be down the hall. Let me know if you need anything!"

"Thanks again!" I called as Leila, Yasmin, and Bear headed down the hall.

"Okay, let me get all this together," Matt said as he piled the counter with towels and a large purple-and-white flat-bottomed tote with compartments full of nail clippers, detangling spray, and shampoo. "If you'll just follow me."

He led us into a room that had a bathtub at waist height and a ramp so the dog could walk up to it. The room was warm and the air was slightly damp, like a bathroom after a shower, and smelled like jasmine. We put on special paw-print oilcloth aprons as Matt showed us how to work the taps, turn on the spray nozzle, and use the blow-dry station. There was another station on the opposite wall, but luckily we had the room to ourselves as we helped Buster into the tub. He was very wiggly, so we clipped his collar to a special attachment that was supposed to keep him from jumping out.

He startled and hopped backward when I turned on the nozzle, so I put one arm around him and sprayed his legs gently. "See? It's not bad."

"Wet dog," Mom said.

"He sure is," I agreed as I sprayed the sides of his body.

"No, I mean, that's step one on this shampoo," Mom said as she studied the side of the bottle. "'Wet dog.' Then 'Lather into dog's fur.'"

"Mom, it's shampoo; we're not building a robot," I told her. "You don't need to read the instructions."

"Just keep the suds out of his eyes," she said.

"He looks miserable." Dickens shook his head. "Poor guy."

Buster has pointy ears that usually flop over at the ends, but now they were pressed flat against the sides of his skull. Tail tucked between his legs, he trembled and looked up at me with big, sad eyes.

"It's okay, buddy," I told him. "Don't worry."

"I always like getting my hair washed at the salon," Sheera told him encouragingly. "It's nice!"

"Why so sad?" I asked Buster as I massaged the shampoo into his fur. "You smell like a strawberry!"

"Maybe he doesn't want to smell like a strawberry," Dickens suggested.

"Who wouldn't want to smell like a strawberry?" I demanded. "This stuff smells better than my own shampoo!"

"At least it smells better than how he smelled before," Mom pointed out. When I frowned at her, she said, "What?"

Dickens started to sing a popular song about smelling like strawberries, and after a moment, Sheera joined in on the chorus. They even managed to harmonize, and I felt a little stab of envy. I don't sing very well.

After three lines, Buster let out a howl and Dickens laughed. "Check out our backup singer!"

"Harry Styles would be so proud," I said.

Sheera beamed. "I think Buster liked it! He seems to have cheered up."

Buster wiggled and seemed nervous, but he mostly

tolerated the shampoo. I put in the conditioner, too, which was coconut, and suddenly we had a dog that smelled like he'd been hanging out on a tropical island cruise.

"Okay? All done," I said as I shut off the spray and unhooked Buster's collar. He stood there, dripping, with his head hung low.

A phone jangled, and my mom pulled her cell out of her back pocket. She frowned at the screen. "It's my boss." Biting her lip, she looked up at me. "Are you guys okay for a few minutes?" The phone continued its cheerful guitar ringtone.

"Sure, Mom, no problem." I waved, gesturing for her to go ahead.

"We got this," Dickens agreed.

Nodding, Mom touched the screen. "Hi, Devon," she said as she pushed through the door. "No, sorry, I'm not at my desk right now. What's up?"

I turned back to Buster just as he gave his whole body a shake, and water droplets flew everywhere, drenching all three of us.

"Revenge!" I said with a laugh as Sheera dabbed at her face with the edge of her scarf.

"Oh, man!" Dickens wiped his face, too. "I'm all the way across the room!"

"Dickens, would you hand me the towel over there?" I asked, turning my back on Buster for one second.

ONE SECOND.

But that's all it took—Buster jumped onto the ramp, ran down, and darted through the open door.

"Shut the door!" Sheera cried, too late.

"Buster!" I called as Dickens and I raced into the entranceway, where my mom was sitting on a bench, scribbling something in a notebook. She looked up just in time to see Buster race past, and her mouth formed a perfect O as I called, "Everything's fine!" and bolted into the hall.

Matt called, "He headed for the yoga room!"

When we reached the yoga room, we found Yasmin holding Buster by the collar as Leila wiped her face with a towel. Several small dogs—including Bear—were racing around, trotting across yoga mats and hopping over legs and arms. Only one woman was lying on the ground with a bichon frise, apparently asleep, lying across her stomach.

"Oh, no," I cried, hurrying over to Yasmin. "I'm so sorry!"

"It's okay, it's fine," Yasmin said, laughing as Buster tried to lick her face.

"This isn't the first time we've had an escape artist," Leila agreed. "Usually, the dogs are trying to get out of yoga, not in."

That was when I noticed that her clothes were covered in water spots. "He got you!"

"You can't work with dogs and expect to stay clean," Leila pointed out. "Bear! Come!" Bear—who had been play-tussling with a terrier—stopped playing and trotted straight to Leila's side. "Okay, everyone, let's gather our partners!"

As I wrapped Buster in a towel, Leila herded the dogs and their owners back into place. I glanced over at the woman with the sleeping dog, who still hadn't moved. "He's deaf," the woman explained. "I'll just let him sleep through it."

Sheera appeared with an extra towel and dried the floor where Buster had been standing. "Thanks, Sheera," Yasmin said. "I can finish that up."

"Let me get him," Dickens said, hauling Buster— wrapped up in a towel—into his arms. Buster wriggled a little, then gave up and licked Dickens's cheek. "Look at this dog, he's grinning," Dickens said.

"He's so proud of himself," Sheera agreed.

"Sorry, everyone," I called as we ducked out the door.

Mom was tucking her phone back into her pocket when we got back to the reception area. "Is he okay?"

"He's fine," I told her. "Just rebellious."

Sheera rolled her eyes. "Please—he interrupted a dog yoga class, not a meeting of the United Nations."

"Who caught him?" Matt asked.

"Yasmin," Dickens replied. "Got him by the collar."

"That's what I guessed." Matt laughed as he leaned forward to smile at Buster. "She's pretty good at nabbing the runaways."

I heard Sheera snort, but she didn't say anything.

Mom shook her head and stroked Buster's wet ear. "Who is going to adopt this naughty old dog?" Mom asked, half to herself, and I felt my heart sink.

After all, Buster *was* naughty sometimes. This dog was supposed to help my mom relax, but so far, he was much better at making a mess. I petted his wet forehead, and he licked my finger.

Like with the garbage, he hadn't been trying to be bad. But he'd managed it, anyhow.

"Well, that was *different*," Yasmin teased as I placed the wet towels into the basket by the front desk.

"I'm so sorry," I told her.

"I'm just playing," she said. "The whole yoga class thought Buster was adorable. He looks great, by the way. Did you trim his nails?"

"Yeah, but he didn't like it much," I admitted. Dickens and Sheera had helped me put Buster under the blow dryer and finish his grooming. He was looking sleek and tidy. Mom had stepped outside to take another call from her boss.

"Buster needs a bow tie," Dickens joked, looking at the display rack. He held up one with purple dots.

"That's adorable," I said.

"They're easy to make, if you know how to sew," Yasmin whispered. "I'll show you."

"Fun!" We bumped fists as Sheera rolled her eyes.

The bell over the door tinkled and a blonde girl and her father walked in. The girl seemed familiar, and when Yasmin said, "Oh, hi, Rachel," I realized it was the girl from the Pie Salon—Yasmin's friend from Greenwood Academy.

"Are you here to pick up Daisy?" Yasmin asked. "I'll get her." She disappeared down the hallway.

"Hi . . . Rachel, right?" Sheera asked, taking a step forward with a little gleam in her dark eyes. "I'm Yasmin's cousin. I think we met at a party last year."

"Oh, yeah." Rachel nodded. "I remember. Yasmin's birthday. Uh, this is my dad."

Sheera introduced us and we all exchanged awkward hellos.

"So . . . you must miss Yasmin, right?" Sheera leaned against the front desk. "Your whole crew."

I narrowed my eyes at her. *What's she fishing for?*

"What do you mean?" Rachel asked.

"At school, right? Now that she's going to Ward?" Sheera pursed her lips and fiddled oh-so-casually with the stack of business cards by the cash register.

"Oh, yeah, of course we miss her." Rachel's voice was stiff and she glanced at her father uncertainly.

I looked over at Dickens to see if he thought this was a strange moment, too, but he was busy petting Buster.

Yasmin appeared with Daisy, who was a very large, fluffy golden retriever. Daisy hurried right over to Buster, and they sniffed each other in a friendly way as Yasmin handed the leash to Rachel. "Back on Friday?" she asked. "I'll let Matt know."

"Sounds good," Rachel's dad said. "Come on, Daisy."

"See you later. Bye, Daisy!" Yasmin called. "Bye, Rach."

Rachel nodded, flashed a glance at Sheera, and said, "Bye" softly as Yasmin headed behind the counter to leave a note for Matt.

"Don't you want to hang out with Rachel a little more?" Sheera pressed. "You barely chatted with her at all."

Yasmin didn't look up from the note she was writing. "I'll text her later."

"You weren't very friendly with her," Sheera pointed out, and Yasmin's head snapped up. Her eyes locked onto Sheera's.

"Why do you care, all of a sudden?" Yasmin asked.

Sheera leaned toward her cousin. "I just find it strange that you weren't nicer."

"That's pretty funny, coming from you," Yasmin snapped. "You've always treated my friends like dirt."

"More like the other way around, *Yasmin*," Sheera shot back.

Dickens looked up from where he was crouched with Buster. "What's going on now?"

"We're leaving," I announced, grabbing Sheera's elbow. "Mom is waiting in the parking lot. Yasmin, thank you so much for letting us come in with Buster! He smells great. And thank your mom, too."

Yasmin tore her eyes away from Sheera's and said, "No problem. I'm glad you brought him in."

"See you at school tomorrow!" I added, calling over my shoulder as I hustled my friends and my foster dog through the door out of Poochalicious.

Mom waved at us from beside the car and said "Okay, thanks so much. Devon wants this by tomorrow morning" into the phone. "I'll call you later when I'm back at my computer." Then she tapped the screen and inhaled deeply.

Sheera was quiet as she climbed into the car. I sat in the front and Buster hopped into the backseat, plopping himself onto Dickens's lap to see out the window more easily. "All in all, I'd say he was a pretty great dog,"

Dickens said. "That place is crazy. I wish Loretta could go to skink day care. Or skink yoga!"

We all laughed then, and the tension in Sheera's face seemed to flow out the open car window.

I had thought she was going to take my advice and try to forgive Yasmin, but I guess she changed her mind. *Maybe she just needs more time,* I told myself. *She'll come around. She isn't as stubborn as she seems.*

DIY: Make Mom More Relaxed

When we got home that night, Mom hopped onto her computer and was there for *hours*.

I had to admit that my brilliant idea to help Mom relax via dog therapy hadn't really gone as expected. In fact, so far, it was seeming more like the opposite.

So I decided that, if Buster was actually making my mom more stressed, then I was going to have to try harder to help Mom relax via Helpful-Child Therapy.

I made a short list of ways I could be more helpful:

Do laundry.

Cook dinner once a week.

Clear my hair products off the sink in the bathroom.

Walk more quietly around the house.

Sweep something (?).

And make sure Buster doesn't bother Mom.

CHAPTER SEVEN

"Okay, Bustie, this is going to be cute." I had placed Buster's dog bed at my feet under my mom's desk in her crafting den. Tuesday night, I looked up how to make a bow tie for a dog, and Mom let me pick out some fabric from her supply. I usually ask her to remind me how to thread the bobbin on her sewing machine, but I am working on the Helpful-Child Therapy, so I looked it up on YouTube.

Now it was Wednesday, and I was sitting down to start the bow tie. Yasmin had messaged me the instructions, and I couldn't wait to see Buster looking dapper in this cute whale-print fabric. I had already ordered the clasps online. "You'll be the best-dressed dog on the block."

Buster let out a loud snore. He wasn't really that into fashion, I guess.

A car door slammed and tires squealed, loud enough to

hear over the gentle whir of the sewing machine. I stopped what I was doing and went over to the front window just in time to see Milton's Toyota reach the end of the block. That stop sign, always slowing him down and ruining his dramatic exit. Buster—who woke up the minute I moved—hopped onto the chair beside the window to see what I was looking at.

I scanned Dickens's front yard and noticed two legs sticking out from beneath the canopy tree. "Stay here a few minutes, Buster," I said, stroking his soft, velvety ear. "I just want to talk to Dickens." Buster looked at me as if he understood. He followed me to the door but didn't try to come with me as I stepped onto the front porch. I turned the key in the lock and walked across the street to sit with Dickens under the tree.

"Knock knock," I said as I parted the leaves. He lifted his head slightly, then let it fall back against the grass. "You okay?"

Dickens stared up at the yellow leaves, which were thick enough to hide most of the sky, like an umbrella casting off rain. There was still light enough to see by, but the weeping branches fell all the way to the ground around us. The canopy tree felt like a tent or the kind of pillow fort you make when you're a kid: cozy and safe from the rest of the world, a curtain between us and the rest of reality.

"My brother is dropping out of college," Dickens said, still gazing straight up. Dickens's chest rose as he heaved in a big sigh.

"Well . . . maybe he just wants to take some time off. Lots of people take time off in college." I leaned back on my elbows, wishing I could think of something more encouraging to say. "Maybe he needs something interesting to do. Like maybe he'll want to volunteer at the shelter?"

Dickens let out this little chuckle. "Rueful" is the word that I think would best describe it. "There goes Goosie, always trying to solve everyone's problems."

"I'm sorry, I—"

Dickens reached out and touched my hand. "I didn't mean anything bad," he said.

I stared down at our hands. His fingers were long, much longer than mine—it was no wonder that he could play the saxophone so well or pluck guitar strings. I'd known Dickens so long and I saw him so often, I never stopped to think about how much we had both grown and changed.

When we were small, we used to hold hands all the time. Our moms had photos—hugging, holding hands, always close.

But we never did that anymore. I wondered when we had stopped as I noticed how warm his palm was, despite the chill in the air, and that I could hear my heartbeat in my ears. "I—"

Dickens shifted to sit up and moved his hand to his lap. "It's okay; I know rescuing everyone is your way of helping."

Something was caught in my throat and I had to clear it as I pushed myself forward into a seated position. "Um, right . . . I'm just . . . well, I guess I *am* trying to solve everyone's problems—catch two birds with one stone. I worry about the animals. Particularly the older ones."

"Still nobody for Buster?"

I picked at a blade of grass. "Nobody's called. I can tell that over fifty people have watched the video I made, but I think they get scared off when they realize he's a senior."

Dickens shook his head. "He's such a cool dog, though."

"I know." I sighed. "But I also feel bad because my mom seems so overwhelmed. I really shouldn't have said we'd foster him for so long. It was just . . . so hard to leave him at the shelter." I tossed away the blade of grass. "You're right—I really do act like I have to save everyone."

Dickens leaned forward, ducking his head so that he could look into my eyes. "I couldn't have done it, either," he said quietly. "Left him there, I mean."

A yellow leaf fell, circling and fluttering, to land by Dickens's knee as he looked at me with that serious, soft, brown-eyed gaze. I think I must have been feeling the way animals feel when they're with Dickens—safe, and valued, and completely understood. It was a warm-soup feeling, a cozy-story feeling, a soft-pillow feeling . . . and it was such a relief after a chaotic week that I leaned forward.

"What are you doing?"

I froze, then sank backward. "I was going to kiss you on the cheek," I admitted. *I think,* I told myself. *I was going to kiss him on the cheek, right?*

"Maybe . . ." Dickens's lips were slightly parted, his eyebrows knit together. "Maybe don't."

My stomach went cold just as my face started to burn. I felt my whole body throb with embarrassment as I realized I had almost done something incredibly, incredibly stupid. "R-right," I stammered. "Right. That was . . ." I gestured wildly, trying to indicate that my brain had left my skull, which might have actually made me look about as delirious as I was feeling. "I was just saying thank you. Awkwardly! Ha! And now it's even more awkward! Yay, nailed it!" *Stop talking!* I commanded myself, but my mouth had already gotten a running start. *If you can't stop talking, then get out of here!* "So, listen, I'll just—" I got to my feet and crouched backward, through the branches.

"Goose—"

"I'll see you later, Dickens."

"Mackenzie—"

"Gotta get back to Buster!" I let the curtain fall between us and hurried back across the street. Dickens didn't come running after me. I knew we'd both have to pretend that this never happened. That would be the best thing—never mention it again.

Buster greeted me when I unlocked the house, hopping around as if I had been gone a lifetime.

Which I kind of felt like I had.

DIY: How to Make a Mess

Ohnoohnoohnoohnoohno—

 Why did I do that?

 What was I thinking???

 I almost kissed Dickens!

 (Did I, though? I was going to kiss him on the cheek!)

 But he thinks I was going to kiss him! Ew! Gross!

 (Is it, though?)

 I'm not really sure if I'm more sorry that I almost kissed him or that I backed out before I did it.

CHAPTER EIGHT

"He really does look handsome," Mom said later that night when I held the bow tie around Buster's neck. "I can't wait for those clasps to come."

"They're supposed to be delivered tomorrow." I scritched Buster behind the ears and offered him a closer look at the bow tie. He gave it a disinterested sniff and then sneezed.

Mom had been watching from her place on the couch, where she was reading some kind of report for work and making notes. Buster hopped up beside her, settling on a pile of papers. "Oh, come on, dog," she said. "Those are important. I swear he can make himself weigh five hundred pounds," she added as she tried to lift him aside.

"That's his superpower," I agreed. I came over to pick him up, but he wriggled out of my arms and strolled over to his bed in a huff.

"This report has a paw print on it." Mom frowned.

"You'll have to tell them that the dog ate your homework."

Mom gave me the dead-eye stare. "Hah. Hah." She sighed. "Well, at least I won't have to worry about it next week."

"Wait—what? Next week? Why?"

Mom tilted her head. "Mackenzie, I told you that Buster could live with us for two weeks. It's already been a week and a half."

"But he hasn't found a home yet," I protested. I looked over at the dog, who had buried his face into the side of his bed.

"I know, sweetheart, but he can't live with us forever," Mom said. "I'm too busy—"

"Just until he finds a home," I begged. "I'm going to help out more. I already have a plan—I'm going to take over the laundry and cook once a week—"

"Mackenzie." Mom put her papers aside and turned to look me in the eye. "That could take months. We talked about this." She wasn't yelling. Her voice was gentle. And she hadn't said anything that I didn't know already, but for some reason, I felt my eyes fill with tears. Buster had to stay with us! My mom *needed* him!

"But he makes you so happy!" I cried.

"Sweetie," Mom said, "oh, sweetie, oh, come on." She wrapped me in a hug. "I care about Buster, but we can't keep him, honey. You knew—"

"I know," I whispered.

"It's hard, but Buster will be okay—"

"It's not just that."

She pulled back and held my shoulders, studying my face. I stared down at the smooth couch cushion. "Do you want to talk about it?"

I shook my head. I didn't want to talk about Dickens or Buster, or anything. I felt like all my words had suddenly dried up and blown away on the wind. I had done too much talking already.

"Sweetheart, it's hard to love someone," Mom said, and I felt like she had just reached into my brain and read it like a page from a book. She looked over at Buster and said, "I love that little guy, too."

"I know you think he's a pain sometimes," I told her. My heart was thudding in my chest. I knew I was doing it again—trying to save someone—but I couldn't help it. I just couldn't.

I could hear Dickens's voice saying *I couldn't have left him there, either,* and our awkward moment flashed across my mind so clearly that it made me cringe.

Mom reacted to my expression and reached to squeeze my hand. "We're all a pain sometimes," Mom said. "That's what love is all about—caring for someone even when they're not perfect. But, sweetheart, I have work. You have after-school activities. You can't give them up forever."

I still thought that there had to be a solution. "Zane?"

"He's not a pet guy," Mom reminded me. "I don't think it's fair to keep asking him to help with Buster. Besides, Buster needs someone who will really adore him. I learned with your father that you can't make someone love a dog."

I drew in a breath, and Mom reached for her glass of water on the coffee table.

"Here, take a sip," she said. "Fairy powers."

Mom always says that water has fairy powers. If you splash it on your face, it wakes you up. A hot shower relaxes you. A sip from a cool glass of water calms you down.

I drank a bit and the fairy powers seeped into me from the inside out.

"When Buster is at the shelter, more people will be able to come and see him in person," Mom pointed out. "It might not be fun for him, but I think he'll have a better shot at finding a home that way. Video is good, but in-person is the best."

I looked over at Buster, who was curled up, snoring softly. "I love his snore."

"I know," Mom said. "So do I. But try not to think about it just now."

"Look, Mom, can't we keep him just one more week? Until Pet-A-Palooza? I'm helping out at that, and I can make sure he finds someone."

Mom was still gazing at Buster. She shook her head, and I thought she was going to say no, but instead her mouth twisted to the side and she said, "Okay. One extra week."

"Thank you, Mom." I gave her a huge hug.

"I think we'll both feel better if we see him go off to a nice home," she added. "I care about him, too, you know."

I rested my head against her neck, feeling a little better. I knew she cared about Buster. But I also knew that she wasn't just doing this for him. She was doing this because she cared about me.

And if there's one thing that can make you feel even better than fairy powers, it's remembering that you're loved.

"Hello?" I called as I pushed through the gate and stepped into Poppy's backyard, which was still bright with blooming yellow and purple mums and red asters. This had been my grandmother's garden, and my grandfather kept it up faithfully since she died. He told me that he loved being surrounded by all those living things that she had planted. He liked to think that the blooming flowers were a way for Grannynanny to keep him company.

It wasn't sad, the way he said it.

I usually come to Poppy's on Thursday afternoons, but today I had also brought Buster along because I'd had a little brain wave. After all, Poppy was living alone, and Buster needed a home . . . so . . . *math*: One dog plus one grandfather equals one fabulous solution for everything! It was so *obvious* that I couldn't believe I hadn't thought of it before.

"Poppy?"

"Back here!" Poppy called, and I heard the sound of glass smashing.

I came around the side of the house and found Poppy on the back patio. He was wearing his gardening pants—olive-colored Carhartts—and a denim button-down work shirt. Poppy always manages to look like a lawyer even though he hasn't practiced law in years. He also had on safety goggles.

"Ms. Miller!" A petite woman with white hair piled in a messy bun and fastened with a chopstick stood beside him. It was Alyce, my finishing school instructor. She was wearing ripped jeans and a Rolling Stones T-shirt, and holding a hammer. She also had on safety goggles. "You're just in time to smash!" She brought the hammer down on a blue-and-white plate, which cracked into several large chunks, then handed the hammer to Poppy. "Not too hard," she said. "We want pieces, not shards. Oh!" She noticed Buster and put down the hammer. "Hello! Who is this?"

I introduced Buster, who jumped up on Alyce's legs. "Oh, I'm sorry!" I gave him a warning glance, like *Be cool, Buster, this could be your big chance*, but he ignored me.

"It's fine," Alyce said. "It's nice to meet you, too, Buster."

"Ah, it's nice to finally see Buster in real life," Poppy said. "Buster, I have seen many photos of you via text. You are much handsomer in person."

I smiled. This was great. I knew a guy like my grandfather couldn't resist a dog like Buster!

"What's going on here?" I looked from Alyce to Poppy, who turned toward the table, which held plates and tiles of various colors and shapes.

"I ran into Alyce about a week ago at the farmer's market," Poppy explained, "and she had been so helpful with that painting at the band fundraiser—"

"You just needed to let go of your inhibitions," Alyce put in.

"So we got to talking, and I mentioned that your grandmother had always wanted a mosaic table . . ."

"And I said, 'Oh, that's easy, I'll show you how to make one,'" Alyce finished. "So now we're smashing some plates."

"That sounds—" I started, but Alyce interrupted, alarmed.

"Ho! What's that dog doing?" she asked. Then she clapped. "Knock it off!"

Turning, I saw that Buster had dug up a red aster plant.

"Oh, dear!" Poppy said as I pulled Buster away. My grandfather went to inspect the plant, which was fully dug up with its roots still attached. Poppy sighed.

"Did he kill it?" I asked.

"I think it can be replanted," Poppy said, looking closely at the roots. "I'll get a spade." He didn't look at Buster, and my heart sank. Buster had found a twig and was chewing it happily, completely unaware that he had ruined everything.

"So what's this doggo's story?" Alyce asked as Poppy disappeared into the shed. "Your grandfather tells me that you're fostering."

"Yeah." I explained Buster's situation as Alyce nodded.

"I've got to say, I love Buster's attitude," she said. "He's a big dog in a little dog body."

"Do *you* want to adopt a dog with an attitude?" I asked hopefully.

"Hah! My cat would slice him to ribbons," Alyce replied. "Selma is a Maine coon cat—she's as big as Buster and dangerously jealous."

"It's not so easy to find a home for an older foster dog," I admitted.

"I know how it is when you get a little gray around your muzzle," Alyce said with a mischievous smile. "Folks don't realize that we've still got a lot of life in us, right, Buster?"

Buster kept chewing his stick as Poppy reappeared with the garden spade. "This shouldn't take long," he said, turning to the aster.

"Mackenzie and I were just chatting about how hard it can be to find a home for an older pet," Alyce prompted. She looked over at me and winked. "Maybe you need a dog, Joe."

"Unfortunately, I'm allergic to dogs," Poppy said as he gently placed the plant back into its hole and scooped earth around to fill the edges.

"You are?" I asked. "I never knew that!"

"Your father always wanted a dog," Poppy admitted.

"He did?" I asked, thinking about my mother's dog, Harpo, and how Dad had never liked him much.

"Well, he always wanted a *puppy*," Poppy said, correcting himself. "But he had to make do with a fish because your grandmother was allergic to cats and I'm allergic to dogs." Seeing the expression on my face, Poppy lifted his eyebrows and asked, "Are you worried that you won't find a home for him?"

"Kind of," I admitted.

Poppy stood up and placed a gentle hand on my arm. "Don't be," he said. "Buster will definitely find a home."

"That's the truth!" Alyce agreed, which made me smile. "And he's a great dog!"

"What about your aster?" I asked.

Poppy didn't even glance at the flower. "We aren't asking the plant's opinion," he said.

"I'll ask around for you," Alyce said. "Joe and I both will, right, Joe?"

"Of course," Poppy said, and I wondered when Alyce had started speaking for my grandfather. *I guess she's that way with most people, but . . .*

"We'll make this into a team project, Mackenzie," Alyce added, and I felt a little better. The ideal situation would be for Buster to stay with me. But if I couldn't do that, I could at least find Buster a home. "We'll find him a home in no time."

"A team project," I repeated. Alyce was right. I'd been doing the thing I always do—trying to save Buster all by myself. I decided it was time to pull in as much help as possible.

We had to get Buster a home by Pet-A-Palooza, and I'd just had a brilliant idea.

CHAPTER NINE

"What's up with the birdseed?" I asked as Sheera shifted a large sack higher onto her hip.

"All the bird supplies are located in the main closet," Sheera explained, "but there's a broom closet right by the bird room that would be perfect. I asked permission to reorganize everything, and Sarah said I should go for it. Oh, and check this out." She dug around in her pocket and fished out what looked like a bunch of stacked Popsicle sticks threaded onto a string. She lifted her eyebrows and looked at me over the top of her glasses, as if she expected a compliment.

"Very nice," I told her. "Um, what is it?"

Sheera rolled her eyes. "It's a bird toy for Albert!"

I laughed. "Your boyfriend?"

"What's this?" Dickens asked, coming up behind me.

My face turned so hot that I thought it was about to start

melting into my neck, like a candle. Nothing would be left but a wick of hair. Oh, no—had he heard me say *boyfriend*? Did he think I was . . . ?

"It's a bird toy." Sheera dangled it, pursing her lips.

"Albert will love it," Dickens said, and Sheera shot me a *told you so* glance right before she turned and headed toward the bird room.

Dickens and I stood there for a moment, perfectly still in the quiet entrance. I turned back to the stack of brochures I had been folding.

"So, uh . . ." Dickens started awkwardly, and I couldn't even bear it.

"No, listen, I'm so sorry about that—I promise that won't ever happen again." I looked up into his face, and his steady gaze sent a pool of gooey warmth flooding into my stomach. "I was just . . . it was just . . ."

"Don't worry. We're good," he said.

Are we? I wondered. But what I said was "No, yeah—yes. We're good."

He nodded, and for a moment, I thought he might touch my arm. Instead he shoved his hands into his pockets. "Because I—"

"Albert loves his new toy!" Sheera singsonged as she walked back into the entrance. She pointed at me and added, "I am the bird whisperer, admit it!"

"I—I—" Half my brain couldn't stop wondering what Dickens had been about to say, and the other half couldn't quite manage to hold a conversation about a bird.

"I'll admit it," Dickens said. "You've really taken over that whole bird room."

For a split second, Sheera's cheeks turned pink. Then she caught sight of someone on the other side of the double doors. "What's *she* doing here?"

"Hell-oooo!" Yasmin called as she strolled in. "Look, everyone's here! Are we ready to make this place *amazing*?"

"I asked Yasmin if maybe she'd like to help with Pet-A-Palooza," I explained to Sheera. "I just thought—well, it could be good exposure for the shop, right? And some of the people who are adopting new pets might want to buy stuff or schedule puppy day care or—"

Yasmin swatted me on the shoulder. "Of course my mom and I are *all in*! Mom loves helping shelter dogs!"

"That was a good idea, Goosie," Dickens said.

Yasmin clapped in excitement. "I'm just here to check out the shelter before the event and see some of the animals. Oh my goodness, this place is so cute! I've never even been out here, can you believe it?"

"Yes," Sheera said flatly.

Yasmin ignored her and went on gushing. "Look at this climbing structure for the kitties! Aww!"

Dickens jerked his thumb over one shoulder. "I've got to get back to the bunnies," he explained. "I've got cages to clean."

"See you later!" Yasmin said, giving him a little wave.

I traced my fingertips across the chipped edge of the counter. "You ready for a tour?"

"Definitely! And look what I brought!" Yasmin held up a large black duffel bag.

Sheera cocked an eyebrow. "A couple of optional outfits in case you need a wardrobe change?"

"Exactly!" Yasmin cried. "Wow, you're good. The dogs must look their best. Check it!" Apparently unaware of Sheera's attempted insult or her frown, Yasmin unzipped the tote and pulled out a tiny green-and-white onesie. "Poochie pj's! I've also got these cute little T-shirts, and I brought some bow ties and even a few dog booties. Oh, and look!" She held out a double-sided clip.

"What is that?" I asked.

"It attaches to the camera." She put down the duffel bag and dug around. After a moment, she came up with a dog treat, which she stuck in the clip. Then she attached the clip to her camera. "The dogs look up at the treat and it's like *Smile for the camera!* And I've got props, too." She held up a rubber toy made to look like a hot-pink high heel. She squeezed it, and it let out a *squeak squeak*. "For a doggie diva! Kenzie told me that photos can help the dogs get adopted," she explained to Sheera.

"This stuff is so great!" I said, pulling a squeaky stuffed carrot out of the bag.

"That's for a more crunchy, organic-looking dog," Yasmin said, wiggling her shoulders. "My mom is so into this idea, Mackenzie. We're going to bring our own grooming booth, too!"

"You'd better run it past the people who are actually in charge," Sheera said, still frowning.

Yasmin waved her hand like she was shooing away a fly. "Mom already talked it over with Sarah. I think they're best friends now. Anyway, we're going to set up in the front courtyard."

"Sounds great!" I said. Even though Sheera did not let out a snort, I felt she really wanted to.

"Do you mind if I look around and take a few photos?" Yasmin asked.

"Sarah might," Sheera snapped.

"Sheera's right. We should let Sarah know," I said. "She's in her office. But I don't think she'll mind."

"She won't like putting the pajamas on the dogs," Sheera insisted. "Some of them are aggressive."

Yasmin rolled her eyes. "I'm not going to dress up any Rottweilers without asking if it's okay."

"It's silly, anyway," Sheera said. "It's deceptive."

Yasmin scoffed. "Deceptive? How?"

"People should adopt the animals for their personalities," Sheera said. "Not because they're dressed up."

Yasmin rolled her eyes dramatically. "Okay, *Sheera*, so how are people supposed to get to know the dogs if they never click on a picture on the website? How are they supposed to love their personalities if they never stop to pay attention to them in the first place?" She turned to me and added, "That reminds me, when we do the grooming at the event, we can brush out the dogs and put little bows in their fur, and—"

This time, Sheera did snort.

"What was *that* for?" Yasmin demanded. "Sheera, do you want these animals to find homes or not?"

"Yes, *and* I don't want them to get returned when they aren't one hundred percent adorable all the time," Sheera said. "Maybe it's good that we're weeding out all the shallow people."

"This isn't about being *shallow*, it's about *sales*. We have to sell these animals. Not, like, literally, but—you know—show them off!" Yasmin gestured to Penny, who was sleeping in her usual spot near the window. "Like this janky old cat. Some random person isn't going to just walk in here and fall in love with him."

"Well, actually—" I began, thinking about Greta.

"You think people will love a cat just because she has a bow on?" Sheera squawked.

"It might help!" Yasmin shook her head. "Believe it or not, Sheera, looks matter. You may not care about how people dress, but other people do!"

With that, Sheera slammed down the stack of flyers and stormed out of the shelter.

Yasmin blinked at me. "What did I say?"

I winced. "You said that Sheera doesn't care about how she dresses."

"What? I wasn't talking about her. She was literally saying that she thinks getting dressed up is shallow!" Yasmin said. "Doesn't that mean she doesn't care about how people dress?"

"She doesn't *care*, but . . . maybe she doesn't want to look like someone who doesn't care."

Yasmin shook her head. "I just really don't get her."

I didn't think Yasmin was trying to be mean, but this was getting worse, not better. "I'll be right back."

"Sheera!" I darted across the parking lot to where she had fled near some trees. The wind picked up the edges of her red hijab, making it flutter at her shoulders. "Sheera, wait!"

Sheera stopped and stood stock-still, but she didn't turn to face me. As I stepped in front of her, she folded her arms across her chest.

"Did you hear what she *said*?" she demanded. "Why didn't you stand up for me?"

"About the dog pajamas?" I asked.

"No! When she was all *Looks matter, Sheera*." She screwed up her face and used a nasal voice. "Like, *You wouldn't know it because you dress like a slob, but, like, people only care about how you look, which is why I wear big long fake acrylic nails and a ton of eye shadow!*"

"I do think Yasmin's nails are kind of fire," I admitted, and Sheera's eyes widened in the universally understood *I'm going to throttle you* glare. "But more importantly, I don't think she was saying any of that about you."

Sheera rolled her eyes toward the clouds. Then she tilted her head and looked at me over the top of her glasses like she does when she's really serious. "Look, you've got to understand," she said. "Yasmin has always been the cool cousin. She has the shiny hair and the trendy clothes. She doesn't have any idea—" Sheera mashed her lips together and looked away.

"Any idea about what?" I prompted.

"Nothing."

"No. Something—what?"

I could see the muscles in Sheera's jaw working as if she was grinding her teeth, chewing on a thought. "It's just that things are easier for her, that's all." We stared at each other, and even if I thought I knew what she was talking about, I didn't want to say so because I didn't want to be wrong. So I waited, and finally, she rolled her eyes and added, "Because I wear a hijab."

"Your scarf is cool," I said quickly. "All your scarves are cool."

"Okay, but not everyone thinks so. People say stuff to me. And they stare."

"Who stares?"

Sheera threw up her hands. "Like that guy at the cash register at Clarkson's. Like those two old ladies at the pie bar."

"What two old ladies?"

With an exasperated snarl, Sheera said, "You didn't even notice them! Of course! Because *they weren't looking at you*, Mackenzie. They were looking at *me*. And it happens *all the time*. And Yasmin has never had to deal with it, and she doesn't even know what it's like, and then she just says stuff—"

"I get it."

"No." She pointed at me like she was stabbing the air between us. "No, you don't get it, and don't pretend like you get it. You have *no* idea. I mean, I know most people are just curious, but some people seem angry, and some people have told me to go home to Iran or Iraq or whatever, and *I'm from here*! I was born in this *town*! And my dad is from Pakistan, not Iraq!" Her eyes dropped to the ground, but I could still feel the heat of her anger radiating in the air between us.

I didn't know what to say. "Is there—is there something I can do?"

She shook her head slowly. "You can . . . you can just know it." Her dark eyes met mine, and she shrugged. "That's all." She rolled the end of her hijab between her thumb and index finger. "I'm doing this because I think it's a good thing to do. It reminds me of my faith. But sometimes I feel . . . judged. And that's a lonely feeling."

"I—" I bit back the words "I get it." "I hear you," I said instead. "That sounds really hard."

She reached out her hand, as if for a high five, but I just pressed my palm against hers and our fingers interlaced. "So when she says stuff about my clothes, that's what I hear," Sheera explained.

"I'm not sure that's what she means, though."

Her right shoulder lifted toward her ear, then dropped. "I know I'm not cool. I mean, she has a point . . . I am kind of a dork."

"No, you're not a dork," I explained slowly. "You're a *nerd*. Dorks have poor social skills and are awkward and rude. Nerds like books and like to draw. And are good at playing the oboe."

For a moment, Sheera didn't reply. The sky dimmed as a fat cloud crawled across the sun. A bird landed on the tree that sat in the concrete planter near the parking lot, and I wondered what the bird thought of the animals in the shelter.

"That's very specific," she said finally.

"That's how I know I'm right," I told her. "You're a nerd. A cool nerd."

"The funny thing is, Yasmin is more like you than like me," Sheera said, shaking her head.

I considered it. "Well . . . in some ways," I admitted. "But in some ways I'm much more like you."

Sheera pursed her lips thoughtfully. "We'll see."

I looked over my shoulder at the parking lot. "So . . . now what? Were you going to walk home from here? Because I think your house is, like, six miles away."

"I hadn't really thought about it much beyond the part where I was going to storm out angrily," Sheera admitted. "I think I was pretty much planning on having you run after me and talk me into coming back inside."

"Okay," I said. I pulled my phone out of my pocket and checked the time. "This can be the part where I remind you that we're only supposed to be here for another forty-five minutes."

"Do I have to go watch Yasmin put those dumb T-shirts on the dogs and stuff?"

"I honestly can't believe that you don't want to do that, but no, you don't. Just stay at the front desk and answer questions, like we're supposed to be doing."

"I can handle that," Sheera said. And that was what I liked about Sheera—she could get mad, but she could also get over it. She burns bright, but she burns fast.

I can be like that, too.

CHAPTER TEN

"Are we grilling tonight?" I asked as the smell of charcoal drifted into the living room.

"I'm trying out this new spice rub," Mom said, pulling a platter covered with plastic wrap from the refrigerator as Buster danced around her feet. "I want to make sure it's good before I serve it to your friend and her family on Saturday."

"Oh, right, the barbecue!" I said. "Are those chicken kebabs?"

"Mmm." Mom nodded, frowning at the chunks of chicken and vegetables that she had skewered onto wooden sticks. "Maybe I should make something easier."

I shrugged. "These look really great."

"I was thinking I'd cook some corn, too. And maybe make a cobbler."

"Don't go crazy, Mom," I said. "I mean, it's not really

like cooking is your forte. I mean—unless we're talking sandwiches."

"Don't forget my Crock-Pot meals." Mom laughed. "Oh, Buster, stop jumping on my legs. I'm going to go stick these on the grill."

Mom stepped through the French doors leading to the backyard and Buster trotted after her, eagerly keeping an eye on the chicken.

My phone chirped; it was my dad trying to FaceTime. I touched the screen and he appeared . . . alongside a very adorable mop-haired golden puppy face. "Say hello!" Dad cried.

"Who is this?" I yelped. "What's going on?"

"This is our new miniature cockapoo, Bilbo!" Dad said. "Say hi, Bilbo! Say hi!" He was holding the puppy under the shoulders and moving him around so that he looked a little like a puppet. With his dark eyes and black nose, Bilbo was just about the cutest dog I had ever seen. Seriously, he could have been a stuffed toy.

Bilbo looked around in confusion, then up at my dad and gave him a lick. My dad laughed. "We just picked him up from the breeder yesterday!"

"From the breeder?" I repeated.

"Tell her about the allergies," said a voice from offscreen. It was Emilio, my step-bother. I mean step*brother* . . . I guess.

"Yeah, yeah—Emilio has some allergies, so we figured we'd better get someone hypoallergenic, you know," Dad said. Bilbo's little legs dangled from beneath his cute round belly as Dad danced him around again. "Cockapoos are supposed to be good for that."

I heard a *thunk* and looked over at the French doors. Buster was pressing his snout against the glass. That's how he lets us know if he wants to come in or go out—by smearing his wet nose against the window. I reached behind myself and flipped the door open. Buster slinked in and trotted over to his bed.

Dad moved aside as Emilio took the puppy and plopped down in front of the screen. He was smiling, which was unusual. Emilio is the kind of guy that lots of girls probably find handsome, with cool hair—swept tall in the middle and tapered on the sides—thick, straight eyebrows, and deep brown eyes. But all I could ever see was that he was *very* full of himself.

"How's it going, having a puppy?" I asked.

"He's great!" Emilio tickled one of Bilbo's floppy ears. "He sleeps in my room. He wakes up all the time, but . . . he's cute. He's named after a character from *Lord of the Rings.*"

"Yeah, I know," I replied. "I saw the movies."

"Oh, right," he said a little too casually. "I forgot there were movies."

See why he's my step-*bother*? He just had to let me know he was talking about the books. So pretentious!

Emilio put Bilbo down on the couch, where the puppy proceeded to snuffle between the cushions in the most adorable way possible. I squinted at the screen. Bilbo was so cute that it was almost physically painful—if I made a video of him for the shelter, we'd probably crash the website because so many people would be trying to adopt him.

I looked over at Buster, who was trying to dig a hole in his dog bed, and sighed.

"Do you ever read fantasy?" Emilio asked.

"What?"

"Fantasy books," Emilio repeated. "Do you ever read them? I'm reading this great book, *Forest of Souls*, right now. You'd like it."

"That's my friend's favorite book," I said, thinking of Sheera. "Fantasy is her favorite genre. I'm more of a non-fiction person."

"Well, you should try this one," Emilio said. "Then we could talk about it."

Talk about it? I wondered what that was supposed to mean. *Why would we want to talk to each other?*

I spotted Mom heading toward the house, and I leaned over to open the door for her. "Listen, I have to set the table," I said. "Congrats on the puppy. Bye, Bilbo! Bye, Dad!" I called.

"Your dad's in the other room," Emilio said.

"Well, tell him bye."

We hung up, and I just sat there for a moment as my mom placed the platter of grilled kebabs on the table, saying, "Voilà!"

"Those look good," I said, but there wasn't any enthusiasm in my voice.

"What's up?" Mom asked. "Everything okay?"

"Oh, I just . . . I talked to Dad. And Emilio. They got a puppy."

Mom gave her head a slight shake. "What?"

"They got a puppy," I repeated. "One of those designer breeds."

"Those dogs cost over a thousand dollars." Mom ran a finger over her eyebrow. "Your dad doesn't even like dogs. Why would he do that?"

"Emilio wanted one. But Poppy said that Dad always wanted a puppy when he was a kid."

"Well, he never liked *my* dog."

And then we both looked over at Buster, who had moved on from digging and was now chewing on his dog bed. He had pulled a lot of the stuffing out already; it looked like he was lying in the center of a snowdrift. When he felt us watching us, he looked up, his eyes bright over his gray whiskers. Then he snuffled and went back to chewing.

We didn't say anything, but I guessed that my mom was probably feeling a little bit like I was—partly annoyed that Dad got a puppy after years of saying no to a dog and not caring about Harpo. And partly annoyed that he got the world's cutest dog and paid a mint for it when he knew that we were fostering Buster. And also . . . a little jealous.

"Well," Mom said at last, "that puppy may be cute, but he's no Buster."

"But Buster isn't actually ours," I pointed out.

Mom sighed. She looked at me, then she looked at the kebabs. "Let's try these before they get cold," she said. So we did.

And even though dinner was delicious, neither one of us said much about it.

When I got home from school on Monday, I went and collected Buster from Zane's place, as usual. Buster usually spends most of his mornings asleep at Zane's feet as Zane writes in his home office. They go for a walk at lunchtime, and then Zane gets back to work and Bustie goes back to sleep. By the time I get home, Buster is ready to play.

"I need a break," Zane said as he handed me Buster's leash. "Were you going to the park?"

"He's been into chasing the ball lately," I said, "so I was going to do that in the backyard. I don't let him off the leash at the park."

"Mind having some company? I was going to pull a few weeds, anyway."

Of course I didn't mind, so we went out to the backyard.

Buster had only recently learned fetch and didn't *totally* get the idea yet. I would throw the ball and he would chase it and grab it, but then he would run all around the yard like a lunatic, hanging on to it for dear life.

I lunged at Buster to get the ball and he darted away, then did a high-speed lap of the whole yard, ears flapping. Zane had been kneeling, pulling weeds from between his bed of somewhat sad-looking mums, but he stood up to let Buster speed by.

"Isn't he supposed to let go of the ball?" Zane asked as I raced after Buster, shouting, "Drop it! Drop it, Bustie!"

"He thinks this is part of the game," I said, panting.

Buster stopped perfectly still, and we squared off. Then I moved toward him and he raced away again.

"Buster, your technique is off," Zane announced. Buster did another lap, then ran up to Zane and dropped the ball, which rolled toward Zane's feet. Buster sat obediently and looked up at Zane. Zane turned to me. "What does he want?"

"He wants you to throw it."

"Buster, go to Mackenzie. She's the one throwing the ball, not me." He crouched back to his flowers, and Buster picked up the ball, stepped closer to Zane, and dropped it right on top of a purple mum.

"Uh, it looks like he isn't going to take no for an answer," I pointed out.

Wincing, Zane picked up the ball gingerly between his index finger and thumb. "This has dog slobber on it."

"Buster isn't a slobbery dog."

"If you say so." Zane looked baffled. "What do I do now?"

"You toss it," I said, making a throwing gesture.

Zane threw the ball. I watched as it sailed over the fence. Buster started after it and then sat, confused.

"Wow, you're really *not* a pet guy, are you?" I said.

"I'm not really a sports guy, either," Zane admitted. "Unless you count watching on TV."

"Hello?" called a voice, and Buster stood up again, butt wiggling as his tail wagged.

"We're out back, Mom!" I shouted, and Mom appeared a moment later. She had already kicked off her shoes and untucked her work shirt, and Buster dashed over, jumping up against her legs.

"Buster, down!" I said, but Mom just patted him. "Mom, your nice work pants."

"Eh, forget it," she said.

"But we're supposed to be teaching him good manners," I insisted.

"Today"—Mom's voice was slow and heavy—"I do not care."

"What happened?" Zane asked.

"Yeah, why are you home so early?" I added, suddenly realizing that she was.

Mom walked over to one of our iron chairs and sat down hard. "My position has been eliminated," she announced.

Little tendrils of cold wound their way around my stomach. "What—what does that mean?"

"I got laid off, Mackenzie." Mom reached absently to pat Buster, who had followed her to her chair and put his paws up on her knees. "I don't have a job. They had security escort me to my car."

"Oh, no," Zane said, "Allison, I'm so sorry."

"You were supposed to get promoted!" I said.

"Well, I had *hoped* so." Mom wiggled her toes. "But instead they eliminated my job and are making this other guy do two jobs." Buster seemed to sense how she was feeling, and licked her ankle.

"This is probably not helpful, but I'm going to say it anyway." Zane walked over and gently brushed my mom's hair away from her shoulder. "It's good that you got out. They were already putting the squeeze on you, and it was only going to get worse."

Mom reached up and held his fingers. "You're right," she said slowly. "That's not helpful."

"Wait, wait—what does this mean?" I demanded.

"It means I have to find a new job."

"But what if you don't?"

Mom looked at me, then stood up and came over to give me a hug. "Don't worry," she murmured into my hair. "They gave me a severance—they're paying me for three months. And I can pick up some freelance work. We'll be okay."

"And you can always go on unemployment," Zane added.

The word "unemployment" made me look at Mom with huge eyes. "I will if I need to," she said simply. "But I probably won't need to. I think I can get a job in three months. But we will need to be a little . . . careful about money."

I glanced at Buster, who had trotted over to the fence

to sniff around for his missing ball. Mom's eyes followed my gaze, and she inhaled deeply, then let out a long sigh.

"You know what?" she said suddenly. "Forget this. I'm calling a Gaga Day."

I was shocked. "Now?"

"We need it."

"What's this?" Zane asked.

"A Gaga Day is when you live like Lady Gaga," I explained. "You put on sunglasses and blast music. And you eat an ice cream sundae for dinner."

Zane looked doubtful. "Is that what Lady Gaga does?"

"It's more like *inspired by the lifestyle of,*" Mom explained. "The important thing is to have fun and be fabulous. But you left out the most important part, Mackenzie."

"Oh, right—you have to make your order really weird," I explained. "Like you have to ask for twelve maraschino cherries."

"Or exactly four rainbow sprinkles," Mom added.

"And maybe Buster can have a bowl of whipped cream or something," I put in.

"Okay, let's go," Mom said.

Zane looked at his watch. "It's only four."

"Time has no meaning!" Mom announced in her most theatrical Lady Gaga voice. "On Gaga Day, it's always fabulous o'clock!"

Zane studied us as Mom and I looked at each other and dissolved into giggles. Sometimes I think I inherited my mom's sense of humor because we crack up at the exact same stuff. "Am I invited to this thing?" he asked.

"All are welcome!" Mom announced, still in her Gaga voice. "But you must wear sunglasses!"

"And be fabulous," I added.

Zane considered it. "I'll do my best."

"You, too, Bustie," I said, and Buster wagged his tail. A Gaga Day. Mom was right: We could all use one.

"Why is Buster the best dressed one of us?" Mom asked as she dug out another spoonful of her sundae, which was topped with only orange M&M'S. "Did you make that bow tie, Mackenzie?"

"Of course!" I said.

"How do you get those glittery things to stay on?" Zane asked.

"They're rhinestones, and I hot-glued them," I told him. "A guy's gotta have some bling."

"Tell me about it," Zane agreed, although he is the least blingy guy in the whole world. He had tried to come along for Gaga Day in a white button-down shirt—his only fancy shirt, he said—so my mom had added a colorful scarf and I gave him my red beret. With the sunglasses, he was somewhat passable, but he had ruined the effect by ordering a vanilla sugar cone and then trying to fabulousify it by asking for a marshmallow on top. He had argued that he was going for something minimalist. He clearly needed Gaga practice.

"I can't believe you actually have dog sunglasses," Mom added. "Where did you even get them?"

"Oh, Yasmin gave them to me the other day. They're called Pet Peepers; they're supposed to keep dust and stuff out of dogs' eyes when they put their head out the window."

"Buster does love to do that," Mom admitted. "And he can roll the window down himself."

"Are those people looking at us?" Zane asked, peering at a group of laughing high schoolers nearby.

"They should be," I said. "We look awesome." Well, I know I did. I had on a black lacy dress, Mom's red cowboy boots, and black sunglasses, and I had used some of Mom's black eyeliner as lipstick. I was having a chocolate sundae with hot fudge sauce and chocolate sprinkles to keep with the dark look.

Mom had gone the other way and was wearing the gold top she usually saves for New Year's Eve with her skinny jeans. Her sunglasses were rose gold, and she had put on every necklace she owned, including the one I had made out of macaroni when I was in kindergarten. "You'd better watch your sugar cone," Mom said to Zane just as Buster made his move.

"Buster!" Zane cried as a long pink tongue knocked the ball of vanilla off the cone and it plopped onto the sidewalk. Buster dove after it, immediately scarfing it up.

"Stop!" I shouted, but Mom just shook her head and held me back.

"It's fine, it won't hurt him," she said. "That crazy dog."

"What about me?" Zane demanded. "What about my ice cream?"

"Just ask yourself WWLGD?" Mom said.

Zane had to think about that for a moment. "What would Lady Gaga do?"

"Get another ice cream," I told him. "And make it even more fabulous this time."

My phone dinged just as Zane went inside to get a replacement. "Oh, hey, look at this," I said, clicking on one of the photos. I held out the phone to my mom. "Yasmin took these at the shelter the other day."

Mom looked down and chuckled at the photo of a dog that looked like a cross between a Labrador and beagle in a striped necktie. Yasmin had added his name, Horatio, and a bunch of cartoon hearts to the image.

"She did this for lots of the animals." I showed Mom a pair of rabbits wearing shirts that made them look like Bert and Ernie from *Sesame Street*.

"Oh, these are so cute," Mom said, scrolling through photos.

"Did I tell you that Poochalicious is going to sponsor the Pet-A-Palooza next week?"

"How are they promoting it?" Mom asked.

"I think they're putting it on their website."

Mom spooned up three M&M'S. "Do they use social media?"

"I'm not really sure," I admitted.

"You know, I could write a press release," Mom offered. "We could probably get some good coverage. I have time now. I could throw together some flyers, too, and some images and messages that people can share on social."

"If you do a flyer, I can get Yasmin's brother, Tariq, to blast it out," I said. I made a mental note to be sure to tell Tariq not to add anything to the flyer. The last time he had "helped out," the event had gotten out of hand.

"Great!" Mom said. "This is definitely what Lady Gaga would do."

"I have returned!" Zane announced as he burst back through the doors that led to the outdoor patio.

"Oh, you got something not vanilla this time!" Mom nodded in approval.

Zane had a bowl of chocolate mint chip ice cream topped with chocolate whipped cream and a whole banana sticking out of the top, like a handle. "I think I'm getting into the spirit of this," he said as he slipped into his seat.

I still thought that Zane's new order needed another degree of Gaga-ness, but he was definitely headed in the right direction.

I held out my phone and showed him some of Yasmin's photos, and we all laughed and oohed over them.

"So you're getting to know both of my nieces," Zane said after a while. "How's that going?"

"Not so well," I admitted. Then I filled him and Mom in about the tense scene at the shelter over the weekend.

Zane sucked a breath through his teeth. "There's a lot of history there," he said.

"It's hard to be friends with both of them," I admitted.

"You know, they're cousins," Zane said, "but even closer than that because they actually live near each other. In a way, they're more like sisters. They fight, but . . . eventually, they always make up."

"I guess they kind of *have* to get along," I said.

Zane took a bite of ice cream and flipped over his spoon to press it between his teeth thoughtfully. "You know . . ." he began after a moment, "I've noticed that they seem to get along best when we're doing something. Like, we all went mini-golfing over the summer, and everyone had a great time. No arguments."

I lifted my eyebrows. "So, like, they get along if they're doing an activity?"

"Makes sense," Mom said. "Maybe you could all work on something together."

"They both like games. Card games, board games." Zane shrugged. "Maybe something like that."

"Hm. Good thinking," I said. "Thanks, Zane." He might not be great at living like Lady Gaga, but Zane did have some good ideas. I needed to get my friends focused on something together instead of focused on each other.

And maybe that strategy would work with Dickens, too. Maybe we could do something together, I thought. *Like hang out at the shelter while we're with the animals. It would be a lot easier to act normal that way.*

I just wanted all the weirdness to pass away. I wanted everyone to get along.

It shouldn't be that hard.

CHAPTER ELEVEN

I woke up suddenly at 11:17 p.m. The only light in my room was the dim gleam of my phone from the bedside table, which lit up my lace curtains with a greenish glow. My heart was beating hard and I had a strange feeling in the pit of my stomach, but I couldn't quite figure out why. Everything seemed normal—I could see the basketful of clean clothes that I hadn't put away lurking beside my bureau, and the usual chaos of half-finished art projects, fabric paint for a T-shirt I was decorating for Buster, and my oboe case lay scattered across my desk. My floor was its normal minefield of dirty laundry and books.

Oh . . . did you think I was one of those tidy people? I'm not.

I had only lived in this room for two months, but I had already managed to make it look as if I had been nesting here for ten years. The mess was boringly familiar. So why the weird nausea?

Mom's solution to my mess is to keep the door to my room closed, but then it gets too stuffy. I like it open, so I always keep it ajar when I'm asleep.

And that was when I realized what was wrong: Buster.

The very first night he was with us, I had cleared up my floor and put his crate with the dog bed in it on the far side of my bedside table. When I slipped under my covers, he had obediently gone inside and curled up in a ball, resting his chin on his hind leg. But I didn't want to lock him inside; I thought he might get thirsty or something, so I left the door open.

That following morning, I'd woken up with a heavy feeling on my feet: a sleeping dog.

Our house can be a little chilly in the morning and a warm dog was a nice thing to have on my toes as I lay in bed an extra few minutes. Since then, I had let Buster sleep with me every night.

But he wasn't here now.

I decided to get up and get a glass of water, and maybe just check on Buster while I was at it. I heard a voice and felt nervous, but the voice was followed by a swell of music and I realized that the television was on in the living room.

Mom was asleep on the couch, her head propped against one of the colorful patchwork pillows she had made. The light from the television flickered across her face. There was a box of tissues on the coffee table in front of her, and scattered tissues on the floor near where her hand was resting. Beside her on the couch, stretched along the length of her chest, was Buster. His head was on her shoulder and he was snoring softly.

The air around me felt thin, my head dizzy. It was pretty easy to read what had happened—my mom had been watching TV and crying about her job, and Buster came to make her feel better. Then she fell asleep petting him.

In movies, people always cover sleeping people with a blanket, but our blanket was folded over the side of the couch and Mom was lying against it. I considered getting a quilt from her room but realized that covering her would probably wake her up. Mom had been smiling and cheerful all throughout our Gaga Night, and I realized she probably didn't want me to see how upset she had been. If I woke her up, she'd know that I had seen the tissues. So I decided to let her sleep without a blanket. After all, she had a dog to keep her warm.

I watched them for a moment. The gray whiskers around Buster's face twitched with each of his soft snores. He might be an ice cream thief, and terrible at fetch, and sometimes a stinky old guy, but he definitely knew how to make my mom feel better. "Good boy," I whispered.

Sometimes, when I'm lying awake, a little worry worm will wiggle into my ear and whisper things to freak out about.

After I crawled into bed, the pit in my stomach wouldn't go away. I started worrying about what would happen if Mom couldn't find a new job. Would we have to move out of our new place? Would I maybe have to go live with Dad and his family in Denver? Would my mom be all alone?

Then I started to worry about Buster. What if he couldn't find a home? Would he live at the shelter for the rest of his life? Would he die there?

I hated thinking about poor Buster's life without us.

Before we came along, he had lived all alone in that garage after his owner had died. He must have been so lonely.

There are so many ways to be lonely in this world.

I hugged my pillow and turned over onto my side. The worry worm quieted down a little, and I breathed in a deep sigh. My mother must have washed my blanket because it smelled sweet and fresh. It was comforting, and smelling it made the future seem further away, and less frightening. It's pretty hard to be scared when you're sniffing the smell of Tide Clean Breeze.

We're all here now, I told myself. *Mom is here. I'm here. Buster is here.*

And tomorrow, you'll work on getting him a home and you won't stop until you do.

CHAPTER TWELVE

"This locker is a special brand of wild," Sheera said as she leaned against the metal wall.

"I know, right?" I agreed as I pulled out my ELA folder. The thing about my locker is that it's the opposite of my bedroom. Maybe because it's just a little one-foot-wide, three-foot-high space, and it seems easy to keep it clean. But to me, locker tidiness is extremely important. I have some shelves and pockets on the inside door for supplies and a mirror and pink-flowered temporary wallpaper at the back, which, okay, is probably a little over the top. But the whole thing makes me happy every time I open that metal door, so it's worth it.

"I want to do mine," Sheera said. "Only with *Spirited Away* art." Sheera's super into old-school anime stuff. Half of the arty kids in our school are really into anime, but I don't know the first thing about it. I like it, though—the whole look of it.

"I'll help," I said. "You can show me some of the stuff you like; maybe we can get some fabric and make an organizer."

"Did someone say 'organizer'?" Yasmin appeared behind Sheera, who gave a little jump.

"Don't just sneak up behind people and chirp in their ear, Yasmin," Sheera griped.

Yasmin held out a box of Nerds candy. Sheera's eyebrows lifted and she took it. "What's this for?" she asked suspiciously.

"Tariq has a bunch of leftover candy. He's trying to convince me to sell it to the upper grades," Yasmin explained. "I told him I needed some free samples."

"You're not actually helping him, though, are you?" Sheera asked.

"Of course not." Yasmin dug around in her bag and pulled out some peanut butter M&M'S. "These are your favorites, right, Mackenzie?"

"Wow, yes! Thanks!" I took the packet and placed it in one of the pockets inside my locker.

"Ooh, cute *and* organized!" Yasmin said with an approving nod. "Anyway, Mackenzie, I wanted you to know that we're all set for Pet-A-Palooza! My mom has been talking with Sarah, and we're going to have a grooming booth and a puppy playground. Mom is heading over to the venue today to take a look. Do you want to come along?"

"Sounds great! I'll have to text your uncle to see if he can keep Buster an extra hour."

"Oh, I'll do it." Yasmin was already tapping at her phone. "He never says no to me." Yasmin looked up from her phone at Sheera. "You can come, too."

The right side of Sheera's mouth curled into a sneering smile. "Thanks. I can't make it today."

Yasmin shrugged, then turned back to me. "Okay. Mackenzie, meet me by the side entrance after school?" Her phone dinged, and she held it up. "He already said yes, so we're all set! This will be so fun!" Then she strutted away down the hall, waving and smiling at everyone. She had only been at the school a couple of weeks, and she already knew more people than I did.

Sheera shook her box of Nerds, listening to the little candies clatter like maracas.

"You should come with us," I said, but Sheera shook her head.

"So that Yasmin can lead me around the place where *I* volunteer? No, thanks. Just—let me know if there's anything I can do for the adoption event."

I wanted to think of the perfect thing to say, but the bell rang, and the noise level in the hall became deafening as everyone started slamming lockers, chatting, and moving toward their classrooms. Sheera shook her box again, then tucked it into the front pocket of her red plaid flannel shirt. "I'll catch you later, Kenzie."

My mouth was dry as I watched her walk away. I felt a little guilty for agreeing to go to the shelter with Yasmin even though I knew it was silly to feel that way. Pet-A-Palooza was super-important, and it was coming up next weekend. And Sheera had been invited along.

I really wished that I could think of something fun that the cousins and I could all do together, like Zane had suggested. Something that felt active; not just all of us being at the same event. *Maybe I can talk it over with Sheera on Saturday at the barbecue,* I thought, and suddenly, it hit me.

The barbecue!

Of course—Zane and Sheera's whole family would be there, and we'd be playing games and stuff. It would be relaxed and fun. And Mom had said that thing about how barbecues are a "more the merrier" situation.

I hurried into homeroom, where Yasmin was already seated in her usual spot. "Hey," I said as I slipped into the seat beside hers, "what are you up to Saturday? Does your family want to come over for a barbecue? Sheera and her family are already coming."

"Sounds fun!" Yasmin said. "What time?"

"Uh, lunchtime—around noon?"

"Great! I'll talk to the fam." Yasmin leaned over and added, "My mom has already mentioned wanting to meet your mom. Like, she's said it about five times."

"Oh, yeah, my mom always wants to meet the friends' parents."

Yasmin laughed. "No, I think it's because your mom is dating my uncle." Then she winked, and my whole stomach felt like a cold, flopping fish.

I hadn't even thought of that.

I just realized that I had invited basically all Zane's

extended family to our house. *Maybe Mom won't care*, I told myself. *Maybe it won't totally stress her out. Maybe it'll all be relaxing and fun.*

Then again, said the voice in my head, *maybe it won't.*

Mom?

Hi sweetie

Don't be mad

Oh no. What???

I invited Yasmin and her family to the barbecue.

Not a big deal

I thought it would be okay because they're the same family as Sheera, technically.

True.

So it's okay?

It's fine! What's the big deal?

Nothing. I just . . . Well, it might be a lot of pressure, because of Zane.

. . .

. . .

Mom?

. . .

Mom?

. . .

It's fine. No biggie! This will be fun.

You're about to throttle me, aren't you?

Yes but I still love you.

That's good. Because I'm not sure Sheera will.

Crinkle crinkle. I studied the toy; it seemed like something a dog would like.

"Here you go, friend!" I handed the toy I had just made to Buster, who immediately chomped on it. I had cut a tie-dyed T-shirt into strips and wrapped them around an empty water bottle, then secured the ends and braided them. Buster lay down on his belly and placed his paws onto the ends of the bottle so that he could gnaw on it more thoroughly. He loves crinkly chew toys. The only problem is that he tears them apart pretty quickly, so I was experimenting with inexpensive options.

"Hey, there!" Mom called as she opened the door. She was holding a brown paper grocery bag, and Zane was behind her with two more.

"Is all that for the barbecue?" I asked, and she grinned.

"Zane took me to the halal butcher! It was a really great store—lots of international foods, too."

"I want to come along next time," I said.

"That's optimistic of you." Zane put his bags down on the kitchen counter. "Are we planning lots of barbecues?"

"Why not? We'll be experts after this one." Mom

shimmied her shoulders.

"You really didn't have to go to all this trouble," Zane said.

"It's no trouble!" Mom insisted, and I'm going to be honest, she sounded a little *too* enthusiastic. I unpacked the bags and she started putting things away.

"Okay, well, I'll see you later." Zane kissed my mom on the cheek and headed toward the door. "I can come over early tomorrow to help out, okay?"

"Sure, sure!" Mom called. "Everything's under control!"

Zane waved at me and ducked out the door.

Mom hummed to herself as she put things into their places.

"How are you feeling?" I asked. "Nervous at all?"

"What is there to be nervous about?" Mom asked. "I'm cool as a cucumber."

"Right," I said. "Okay, but you just put the rice in the fridge and the meat in the cupboard, so . . ."

Mom stopped in her tracks on the way to the fridge. The bag of green peppers swung slightly as she glanced over at me. "I did?"

"May not be the best place for the meat," I suggested.

Blushing slightly, Mom smiled. "I guess maybe I am a little nervous."

"Well, that's good, because *I'm* a little nervous!" I admitted.

We both laughed. Mom put a hand to her forehead and said, "Mackenzie, what was I thinking?"

"And what was *I* thinking?" I demanded.

"Yes, what *were* you thinking?"

"I have no idea!" I pointed at her. "But I *always* do stuff like this, and you *never* do!"

Mom lifted her eyebrows and stuck out her lip, nodding. "True."

"It's just a barbecue," I said.

"It's just a barbecue," she agreed. "We'll grill things. We'll throw a Frisbee."

"It'll be fun," I said. "Right?"

Just then, Buster returned, proudly holding what was left of his new toy: the fabric. He had managed to chew the bottle free, and if I had to guess, I'd say it was probably now somewhere under the couch. "You're pretty proud of yourself, aren't you, Buster?" I asked, thunking him on his solid side. "You liked it so much you went and made a big mess!"

Mom laughed as she pulled the meat out of the cupboard. "I know the feeling," she said.

CHAPTER THIRTEEN

Mom used a spice rub on the meat and let it sit in a Ziploc bag overnight. In the morning, I made a batch of brownies and decorated them with frosting and sprinkles. Then I helped chop vegetables and arrange them on skewers along with the meat while Mom made German potato salad (no mayo), husked corn, and fruit salad. She had decided to skip cobbler; Veena had said that she would bring a dessert, and that along with my brownies would be plenty.

We were lucky with the weather. October can get cold where we live, but the chilly wind had moved through and it was sunny with a high of seventy-five degrees. The barbecue was supposed to start at twelve thirty, but Zane arrived at eleven thirty to light the charcoal and help put out plates.

"What are you doing over there?" he asked as I dragged the large plywood box near our oak tree.

"It's a game called cornhole," I explained. "You toss beanbags from over there, and if one lands on the board, you get a point. If it goes into the hole, you get three points." I dropped the beanbags beside the box.

"This could be interesting." When I lifted my eyebrows, he added, "My family can get pretty competitive."

"You said your family gets along when they're doing an activity!"

"Yes," he agreed quickly. "Usually." He seemed to think for a minute. "And sometimes it gets dangerous."

The platters were arranged on the kitchen island, with Mom frowning at them as we walked back inside. "Do you think there's enough food?"

"Seems like a lot," I said.

"These people can eat," Zane put in. "My brothers especially."

Mom's eyes widened. "So you don't think there's enough?"

"I'm sure there is." Zane shrugged. "And if there isn't, we'll order pizza."

Mom looked horrified. "We can't eat pizza!"

"Why not? Everyone likes pizza," Zane said with a laugh.

"Because we are having a home-cooked meal, that's why." Mom shook her head and I saw her glance at the magazines she had bought at the supermarket last week. Three of them were fanned on the coffee table; the top one showed a platter with a perfectly brown roasted turkey surrounded by delicious-looking roasted vegetables under the headline "Fall Comforts." I think the magazine layout was more the vibe she was going for . . . Pizza just doesn't photograph well.

The doorbell rang.

"Are you ready for the chaos?" Zane teased as my mom opened the door.

"A salaam aleikum!" A round-faced man with thick, spiky black hair and eyes as bright as polished stone walked in with his hand outstretched. "Hello! So nice to meet you! I'm Rizwan and this is my wife, Veena. Ha! Mackenzie, how are you? How are you? Hello, Zane *bhai, a salaam aleikum!*" He was beaming and vibrating with cheerful energy.

"Wa aleikum a salaam," Zane said. "Veena, how are you?"

Sheera's mom, who wore a flower-petal pink hijab with a long sand-colored tunic and matching loose pants, balanced a covered platter on one arm. She greeted my mother with a shy smile and a handshake, then turned to give me a one-armed hug. The family began to spill into our house—all of them at once—like water bursting a dam. In came Sheera looking like a smaller, slightly punk version of her mother. Right behind her was a tall, lanky, serious-looking boy with unruly black hair and glasses—Sheera's older brother, Wali. He was holding the very sticky-looking hand of a little boy with huge eyes—Sheera's little brother, Osman, who immediately spotted Buster and headed over to make friends.

Then came Yasmin, bright and bubbling, followed by her little brother, Tariq, who handed my mother one of his famous business cards and gave me a fist bump. Leila greeted my mother like an old friend, and introduced her husband, Zane's other brother, Aysar. There were dark circles under his eyes and his hair was receding, and he looked like a businessman who worked far too hard. Still, when I introduced myself, he laughed and said, "Ah, the famous Mackenzie," and his eyes were warm when Zane introduced my mom.

I peeked out the front door and saw that there were two vehicles parked on the street. One was a silver minivan, the other was a red BMW. It was pretty easy to guess which car belonged to which family.

Soon, the volume in the house was deafening, and Zane headed to the rear French doors so everyone could start spilling into our backyard. Mom was smiling as she carried a platter of kebabs out to the grill, but I could tell that she was a little overwhelmed. As I mentioned before, she isn't really a party person.

I, on the other hand, thought it was awesome!

Mom, Zane, and his brothers gathered around the grill to do that thing that grown-ups do, where they argue about the best way to cook stuff.

"Hey, do you have any games?" Wali asked. He was holding Osman, who buried his face in his big brother's neck.

"Sure!" This was just the opening I wanted. I led them over to the cornhole setup.

"What's this?" Sheera asked, and I explained about the tossing and the points system. "There's more official rules, but we don't really have to worry about them."

"Oh, I am excellent at games like this," Yasmin announced. "Gimme those beanbags."

"It's about to go down," Sheera told her, motioning for me to give her the other set.

"Okay, so how about teams?" I asked. There was a brief argument, as both Sheera and Yasmin wanted Osman on their team. "Okay, fine," I told them, "then you're on the same team. I'm with Wali and Tariq."

Both Sheera and Yasmin looked shocked, but Tariq high-fived me. I volunteered to go first since I was the only one who actually knew how to play. The first beanbag I threw landed on the board. One point. The second one went in the hole—three. And the third one . . . was grabbed out of the air by Buster, who ran around the yard with it.

Osman screeched with delight as I raced after Buster. The other kids joined in the chase, but Buster was too fast.

"Buster! Buster, come!" Zane called, and Buster dashed toward him. Zane reached into his pocket and pulled out a dog biscuit. "Drop it," he said, and Buster dropped the beanbag at his feet.

"Wow," I said as Buster took the biscuit. "When did you teach him that?"

"Oh, we've been working on it," Zane admitted. "In the mornings."

"What a good dog," Veena said.

"He's up for adoption," Mom said brightly. She took several beef kebabs off the grill and placed them carefully onto a platter that was resting on a low table to her left. Buster's nose twitched, and then several terrible things happened in slow motion: Buster lunged at the table, I let out a shout, Aysar jumped backward, and Buster tipped the platter onto the ground, grabbed a kebab, and tried to lurch away.

Sheera leaped into his path and Yasmin grabbed his collar. Leila dropped her glass of lemonade and shouted, "Don't let him eat the skewer!"

Buster snarled as Sheera pulled the kebab from his jaws. Yasmin released him and Sheera stood up, saying, "Naughty dog."

Buster gazed up at the kebab in her hand and then sat on his haunches, still staring at the meat expectantly. Like he was going to get a treat after that.

And then everything was totally quiet.

I looked over at my mom, who was staring at the scene— Yasmin's white tunic smeared with paw prints, Sheera holding the kebab over her head, the dropped lemonade that had landed all over Veena's shoes. And fifteen beef kebabs in the dirt.

"Oh, no, the kebabs!" Leila cried.

Mom's eyebrows pulled toward each other and her lips mashed together. Her chin dimpled and I could tell that she was holding back tears.

"It's okay, it's okay," Zane said, grabbing her hand. "Don't cry."

"These things always happen," Rizwan put in cheerfully. "Don't worry!"

"Remember the time Osman threw up the Doritos on Aysar Taya's rug?" Sheera asked.

Tariq clutched his stomach. "That was so nasty. Bright orange barf on a white rug!"

"And after we cleaned it up, we looked over and he was back to eating the Doritos?" Yasmin put in.

"Today, we'll just order pizza," Zane said.

"But—I made everything halal," Mom sputtered.

"Pizza!" Osman cried, and Rizwan said, "Really, it's his favorite thing," and everyone agreed, and before there was time to do anything Aysar had whipped out his cell phone to order with help from Sheera—who seemed to know what toppings everyone liked—and Leila appeared with a garbage bag so that she and Rizwan could clean up the mess.

"Look, there is potato salad and regular salad," Veena said. "We have plenty to eat!"

Yasmin helped me bring Buster inside and get him settled with his antler in the living room. We left him there, happily gnawing away, and headed back out.

Mom was sitting down with a glass of lemonade in her hand, and everyone was eating the *sohan halwa*, which was what had been on the covered platter Veena had brought. "Try this!" Tariq insisted, handing me a square.

I took a bite, which dissolved in my mouth with a milky sweet pistachio flavor. "Wow, delicious!"

"My aunt's specialty," he said, then lifted his eyebrows. "Hey, maybe I should start selling these."

"I got out the desserts first," Veena explained to my mom. "I thought people were getting a little hungry. You don't mind?"

"No, no—" Mom looked around. Zane and his brothers and sisters-in-law were all clustered around her, smiling. "This is lovely," she said at last.

"Hah! What a rascal of a dog!" Rizwan slapped his knee. "He has the right priorities," he added, patting his belly.

Aysar held up his glass of lemonade, like a salute. "You have to respect a dog like that."

Everyone laughed, and soon we had started up the cornhole game again. Sheera and Yasmin were extremely competitive, and I was glad that I had put them on the same team. All in all, the barbecue was looking like a success.

Tariq had just landed seven points—two in the hole and one on the board—and went to retrieve his beanbags when Sheera led Osman to the line.

This was Osman's third turn. So far, he had landed two beanbags about five feet beyond the cornhole board, one to the right of it, one to the left, and two about a foot and a half in front of it. It was actually impressive how many spots he had covered without landing any on the board or in the hole. It was fine, though; he was so little. "Okay, now remember, bend your knees before you throw," Sheera said. "No—wait!"

Osman had already let his beanbag fly while Tariq still had his hand in the hole.

The bag landed with a thud on the board as Tariq pulled his hand out. The bag slid off the board and landed with a plop.

"Hey!" Sheera shouted. "Put that bag back on the board."

"No way," Tariq said.

"Yes!" she insisted. "Osman gets a point for that!"

"It fell off!" Tariq insisted. "I didn't get a point when my bag fell off!"

"You jiggled the board." Sheera planted her hands on her hips. "Besides, Osman is *five*."

I looked over at the grown-ups, who were ignoring us. I guessed they'd heard it all before.

"I did not jiggle the board," Tariq said. "Come on, Mackenzie, back me up!"

"Just do it over," I suggested, but Sheera snapped, "No! Osman finally got a point, and it's not fair that this cheater—"

"Hey!" Yasmin held up her hand. "Whoa. Tariq is not cheating."

"He always cheats, Yasmin!" Sheera cried. "And you know it!"

"Chill out, Sheera," Wali said as Osman started to cry.

"He does not cheat," Yasmin insisted. "I'm sorry that not everyone can be a perfect genius like you!" She threw down the other two beanbags and stormed over to the house.

"Where are you going?" Sheera demanded.

"To the bathroom," Yasmin shouted. "Do I have your permission? Is it okay with you?" And she turned her back on us to stomp inside.

Rizwan caught Sheera's eye and called, "Drama?"

Sheera waved him off as Wali sighed. "Nice going," he said to his sister as he picked up Osman.

Sheera took a step toward the rear door, but I stopped her. "Just wait here a minute," I said. "Let me talk to her."

She hesitated a moment, then nodded, and I followed Yasmin.

I waited until she came out of the bathroom, of course. The edge of her hairline lay damp against her scalp, as if she had splashed water on her face. She looked surprised to see me in the hall and said, "What's up?"

"I just wanted to make sure you're okay."

Yasmin shook her head, then gave a half-hearted shrug. "I guess," she said. "It's just—I don't know what's wrong with her. She's so smug and superior . . . like, I thought that once I came to Ward, we'd be friends again. But I feel like she's dumping me."

"Dumping you?"

Suddenly Yasmin looked past me and I turned to see Sheera standing at the end of the hall. I wasn't sure how much she had overheard . . . all the worst parts, I guessed.

"How can you say that after *you* dumped *me*?" she said to Yasmin. "And then dumped your friends at your old school? Watch out, Mackenzie, you're next!"

"That is so rude," Yasmin snapped back. "I don't dump people, Sheera."

"You left your old school and never looked back!"

"You think I wanted to leave? I *had* to leave! My grades were tanking." Yasmin's face burned red, but I wasn't sure if she was embarrassed or furious. Or both. "My mom said that if I couldn't pull my math grade up to a C, she'd yank me out and make me go to Ward."

Sheera folded her arms across her chest. "So why didn't you try to pull up your grade?"

"I did try! I was studying all the time, and then, guess what? My friends stopped inviting me to hang out." Yasmin ran her fingers through her hair as if she wanted to pull it out. "They were constantly posting photos of all the fun stuff they were doing. Then Rachel said that I was no fun anymore. I felt like I had to choose between my grades or my friends."

"So you chose your grades," Sheera said.

Yasmin let out an exasperated sigh. "Are you crazy? No! I chose my friends! I started hanging out and going to parties again, and when Mom saw my terrible grades, she did what she said she was going to do. And now I'm at Ward."

The cousins stared at each other.

"She also said I could start over, and that you'd be a good influence, if I could just try to act more like you," Yasmin finished. Her voice sounded deflated, tired, like a balloon at the end of a party.

None of us knew what to say for a minute after that. I can't imagine how it would feel to have your mom pull you out of school and then put you in a new one. How hard it must have been to hear how much better your cousin was than you.

"That's . . . weird," Sheera said at last. "You don't need me. You're smart."

Yasmin curled her lip and looked at the floor. "Am I?"

"You're smart in ways that I'm not. You're *people* smart."

Yasmin tossed back her hair. "Yeah, maybe."

"No, I mean it. Like—I'm book smart, but you're people smart. Did you know that the shelter has already placed three of the animals that you dressed up in those little outfits? Some of those guys had been waiting for homes for *ages*."

"Oh, no, they didn't tell me," Yasmin said faintly. "That's great. Helping you two with the shelter has been . . . it's been really great."

"You're awesome with the animals," I told her. "And you're fun!"

Sheera nodded. "But . . . can I just say that I can't believe your old friends did that to you? Like, that they didn't support you when you needed to pull up your grades?" She took a step forward and for a moment it looked like she might try to hug her cousin. In the end, though, she just planted her hands on her hips and declared, "That's terrible."

"That's what I realized, too. They weren't who I thought they were." Yasmin pursed her lips. "Or, actually . . . maybe they were. Maybe I just didn't think they'd be that way with *me*. But I don't know why I thought that; I knew what they were like."

"Well, you're with us now." Sheera said it like it was an announcement; like she had decided and it was final. She looked at me, her brown gaze firm. "Right, Kenzie?"

"Yeah," I said. I smiled at Yasmin, who managed to smile back. "You're with us."

"Is someone strangling a cat right now?" Sheera asked as a loud screech interrupted the opening credits of the movie. We all turned away from the TV to look toward the front window.

It was five o'clock, which meant that Sheera, Yasmin, and I had spent the whole afternoon together. The barbecue had gone on and on, with the grown-ups chatting and the rest of us playing cornhole, then catching a Frisbee, then playing ludo—a game that Osman had insisted they bring with them. It was a bit like Sorry, and we had to play in teams, and of course we let Osman win, although Tariq tried his best to beat everyone.

"Next time, we play Monopoly," Tariq insisted. "Nobody ever beats me."

"You'll want to, though," Sheera put in. "You'll want to beat him to a pulp. He's impossible."

Then everyone—including Buster—went for a walk in the park, and by the time we had gotten back, we got the parents to agree to let Yasmin and Sheera stay for a sleepover.

"This never happens!" Sheera cried happily once her parents were gone.

"It's because I'm here," Yasmin said. "I'm a good influence."

We all laughed at that.

"And Zane Chachoo is next door," Sheera added. "I think my parents feel better knowing my uncle is so close by."

"Your parents don't think sleepovers are safe?" I asked.

"They don't like the idea of me staying at a stranger's house," Sheera explained. "They're very into 'risk management.' That's actually what my father does for a living."

"What . . . is it?" I asked. "What does that mean?"

Sheera shrugged. "I have no idea."

"It means he's as overprotective at work as he is at home," Yasmin explained.

"Yes," Sheera agreed, "that."

There were a few kebabs that didn't fall on the ground in the Great Barbecue Disaster, so we decided to eat those for dinner while we watched a movie. And that's when we heard . . . the noise.

"It's horrible!" Yasmin grimaced and put down her kebab.

"We might have some sauce or something," I said.

"No, I mean that sound!"

"Oh, that's just Dickens's band," I told them. "They usually practice at Orlando's house, but they end up here once in a while. They're actually not bad . . . usually."

"Should we go say hi?" Yasmin asked, slipping her feet back into the shoes she had kicked off.

"What—now?" Sheera touched her scarf self-consciously. "Like, at night?"

Yasmin gave her a doubtful look. "It's still light out."

"The sun's going to go down in fifteen minutes!" Sheera said.

Her cousin planted her hands on her hips. "How do you even know that?"

My heart was thudding in my chest. I really wanted to see Dickens in that way that you want to poke at a sore spot on your arm to see if it's better yet. Maybe watching him do his thing in his rock band would seem normal. "I think we can go over," I said. "It's right across the street. Mom?"

My mom had just wandered into the kitchen and she wandered back out when she heard me call. "What's up?" She had changed into her slippers and pajamas already.

"Can we go over to Dickens's house?"

"Sure, of course," Mom said. "Have fun. I'm not going anywhere. Buster and I are going to get in bed and read a book, right, Buster?"

Buster hopped up onto his hind legs and laid his front paws against my mom's shin, giving his back a deep stretch.

We popped on our jackets—Sheera's dad had dropped off backpacks full of clothes, jackets, and pillows for the cousins—and headed outside.

Dickens's open garage door framed him on guitar, Martin on bass, and Orlando on drums. They were just wrapping up a pretty confused, possibly ironic version of the *Friends* theme song when we stopped in the driveway.

When they hit the last note, we broke into applause, and I shouted, "All right, Jonah's Brothers!"

"Wait—you named your band after the Jonas Brothers?" Yasmin asked.

"No, it's a joke—it's actually Jonah," Dickens explained. "Orlando and Martin have a brother named Jonah. So. Jonah's brothers?"

"Is anyone going to get that joke?" Sheera asked. "And isn't Nick Jonas going to sue you?"

"And beat you up?" Yasmin added.

"It's a temporary name," Dickens explained. "Until we think of a real one."

"How about Starbucks?" Yasmin suggested. "Or Snickers Bar?"

"Yeah, how about Billie Eilish?" Sheera put in. "Is that taken?"

"Hah. Hah," Martin said. "Hilarious."

"Listen, forget the name," Orlando said. "What we need is a singer. Martin sounds like a cat trying to gargle with Listerine."

"Shut up, man," Martin told him. "Worry about your own struggles with those drums."

Orlando ignored his brother. "What about you, Mackenzie? Do you sing?"

"Sheera does," Yasmin said.

"You do?" Orlando asked, looking surprised.

"Well, I mean, anyone can sing," Sheera mumbled. Her face was bright red.

"You sang with me," Dickens pointed out. "When we were at Poochalicious, remember?"

"Kind of," Sheera admitted. "I mean, that wasn't really singing."

"Well, come up here, then," Orlando said, waving at the microphone stand. "Show us what you got."

I still felt really awkward, and I wanted to show Dickens that I could be helpful, and not in an I've-Got-to-Save-Everyone way. I could be good old Goosie, the regular friend.

"Just do something simple," I whispered to Sheera. "It'll be fun!" I gave her a little nudge and she stumbled toward the microphone, glowering at me.

"So, we're writing some of our own stuff." Dickens walked over to Martin's mic and adjusted the height. "But we're also playing some covers. Do you know that old song 'Stand by Me'?"

Sheera nodded. "Yeah. I know it."

"Guys?" Dickens asked.

Orlando nodded and Martin said, "Got it."

"Okay! Let's try it out." Dickens went back to his guitar and slung the strap over his shoulder. Orlando held up his sticks and clicked them together to count the rhythm. Dickens strummed the first chord. Then Sheera closed her eyes.

Sheera's voice was not what I expected. She's a small person, slender and about an inch shorter than me. But her voice seemed like . . . like a separate thing. It seemed too big for someone so physically small to be able to make. It was as if it were passing through her and spilling out into the night like a wave, or a cloud. Her voice dove and soared, lingering on some notes and settling them inside me. She didn't even need the microphone.

Her glasses glinted in the fluorescent light as she held the last note. Her eyes were still closed—they had been closed the whole time.

The band stopped playing, and everyone stood perfectly still for what felt like a full minute. I looked over at Yasmin, whose eyes were filled with tears. Finally, Sheera opened her eyes and looked around. "Was that okay?" she asked, like she truly didn't know.

"That was really amazing." Dickens stood up slowly, repeating, "You were amazing."

There was something about the way that Dickens said the word "amazing." It made the center of my stomach turn to ice. After a second, I noticed that Sheera was looking at me, but I still couldn't move.

"You have to join us for the talent show!" Orlando crowed. "With that voice, we're totally going to win!"

"I . . ." The bright red dots had appeared on Sheera's cheeks again. "I'm not sure."

"What's to be not sure about?" Orlando demanded. "You have to!"

Sheera's eyes flashed. "I have to think about it."

"You don't have to think about it," Orlando shot back. "You want to do it or you don't—just give us an answer."

"Okay, then, no."

"How can you say no?" Orlando demanded.

"Orlando, chill out," Dickens insisted. "Sheera doesn't have to join the band."

"I thought she was good," Martin put in, about three minutes behind the rest of the conversation.

"Look, it's getting late." Sheera released the mic and stepped toward Yasmin. "Thanks for letting me sing with you guys." She motioned toward me and Yasmin, and snapped, "Let's go."

"Just think about it!" Dickens called as we walked away.

I turned and tried to gesture something to imply that I would help to convince her, but I think it just came off as pointing and waving. Dickens's expression was blank; I don't know if he got what I meant.

When we reached the house, Yasmin stopped on the bottom step and blocked our way. "You should really think about it," she told Sheera.

"I don't know." She glanced over her shoulder. "Orlando is kind of bossy. And I don't think my parents will want me hanging out with a group of guys all the time."

"Don't your parents want you to do lots of extra-curricular stuff?" Yasmin asked.

"I don't think this is what they had in mind," Sheera admitted. "But . . . maybe."

Yasmin rolled her eyes. "What do you think, Kenzie?" she asked. "You've been quiet."

I knew I should tell her to go for it. *This is my moment. I gave Dickens those encouraging hand gestures!*

But then I remembered Dickens's voice when he said "amazing."

"You should do what you think is right," I heard myself say. "Whatever you think is best. Like, maybe don't rush into it."

Sheera nodded. "Thank you, Kenzie." Then she gave Yasmin a little nudge and stomped into the house.

Yasmin threw up her hands. "Ugh. She's impossible," she said, then followed.

I cast one last look over my shoulder. The guys were standing around, chatting. Dickens looked up at me and nodded, then turned back to argue with Orlando.

A wind blew icy air through my jacket, matching the cold that had settled in my stomach. I walked up the steps and went inside.

CHAPTER FOURTEEN

"What are you girls up to?" Mom asked a few hours later. "Should I make popcorn?"

"Definitely," I told her as I clicked pause on the remote. "We just started the next movie."

"I love popcorn," Sheera said, running a hand through her shoulder-length black hair. When we had come back from Dickens's house, she had taken her scarf off and tucked it into the backpack her father had left by the door. It had surprised me to see her hair. It was so pretty around her face. Still, I didn't say anything about it; I didn't want to make it into a big deal. But I felt like our friendship had definitely gone up a notch, like I was seeing a secret that she didn't share with just anyone.

"I'm going to get my nail polish." Yasmin hauled herself off the couch and walked toward the bags.

"Will you do mine?" I asked, spreading my fingers.

"And mine?" Sheera asked.

"Of course," Yasmin said. "I don't mean to brag, but painting nails is kind of my superpower."

"Could you also let Buster into the yard?" I asked. "He's scratching at the door."

"Sure. Here you go, buddy."

A second after Buster slipped out, we heard frenzied barking.

"That dog," Mom grumbled, heading for the door.

"What's going on?" I asked, following her.

We all stepped onto the patio just in time to see Buster in a face-off. He was barking madly at an enormous raccoon, which was standing on its hind legs and holding a pizza crust that must have fallen from someone's plate that afternoon. It let out a hiss.

"Stay back—" I held up an arm to block Yasmin and Sheera.

"Oh my—"

"What is—"

Zane came through his door at the same moment and stopped when he saw us. Buster was still barking, holding his ground. The raccoon seemed undecided about whether to finish his pizza, deal with the dog, or retreat.

"That raccoon could have rabies," Zane said. "Buster, NO!"

"I don't—" Mom started, but Buster lunged, snapping at the raccoon, and Zane lunged at Buster. The raccoon raced over to the oak tree and climbed to the lowest branch.

Zane scooped up Buster, who wriggled in his arms. Buster was about twenty-five pounds—not huge, but pure muscle, and he was focused on that raccoon, barking and snarling, twisting to get at it. "Buster!" Zane shouted. "Buster! *Ow!*"

Zane fumbled Buster but didn't drop him. He kept one arm wrapped around the dog while he held out the opposite hand, which had a bright red, angry bite mark on it.

Mom gasped. "He *bit* you?"

"Not hard," Zane said. "He just surprised me."

"You're bleeding!" I said.

Zane looked at his hand, obviously still shocked. "It's just a scratch."

Buster had stopped wriggling and was looking up at

Zane with huge eyes. He licked Zane's jacket sleeve; I guess it was the best he could do.

"It's okay, buddy," he said gently. "You didn't mean to."

The raccoon waddled along the length of the tree and jumped to the fence. Then he raced to the end and escaped into our neighbors' backyard.

Buster let out a final bark, and I realized I was shaking. "Mackenzie, are you okay?" Mom asked, putting an arm around me. "Don't cry—it's okay. Buster isn't hurt."

"It isn't that," I said, swiping at the tear that had snaked down the side of my face.

"What's up, then?" Mom asked.

"Even the raccoon is okay," Sheera pointed out.

My throat was so tight that I couldn't force out the words. I waved in Zane's direction.

"What, me?" Zane asked. "I'm fine! We'll just clean up this scratch."

"We know that Buster doesn't have rabies," Yasmin put in. "He's got his tag."

"No," I said. "But he *bit* you, Zane. Don't we have to tell the animal shelter? Don't we have to let them know that he's aggressive?"

"It's just a little scratch," Zane said. "He didn't mean to do it—he was going for the raccoon."

"I think we have to—" I started.

Zane shook his head. "No, look, don't do anything yet. That is—let's do one thing. Let's call Animal Control and let them know about the raccoon, okay? Because he's been here before, and I don't want Buster to get in another animal argument."

"Zane, Mackenzie's right," Mom said gently. "We do have to let Sarah know. Hope House will have to tell prospective adopters."

I felt a hand on my shoulder and looked over to see Sheera's eyes, full of concern. I knew we were thinking the same thing: Buster might never find his forever home now.

"No, but—it was an accident. It was my fault. I shouldn't have grabbed him." Gently, Zane set Buster down on the ground, and Buster shook himself all over and walked around a bit before coming back to Zane and flopping over to roll onto his back. "It's okay, buddy," Zane said, kneeling down and rubbing Buster's tummy. "We're still friends."

"Are you . . . are you worried about Buster?" I asked, watching Zane rub Buster's ears.

"He deserves a good home," Zane insisted. "And this is my fault, not his." Zane looked so guilty and worried that I didn't have the heart to argue with him.

I looked at Sheera, then Yasmin, who gave her head a little shake. Then I turned to my mother, unsure what to do.

"Zane," Mom said at last, "I'm telling Sarah. We'll explain that he wasn't being aggressive, but they really have to know that this happened. It might hurt Buster's chances, but we don't want to put anyone in danger, either."

Zane squeezed his eyes shut and shook his head slowly. "Don't do it."

"I have to."

Pulling himself to his feet, Zane took a deep breath. Then he went back through the door that led into his side of the house.

My mother watched him walk away, then folded her arms across her chest and rubbed her shoulders. "It's getting cold. Let's go inside."

I walked over and gave her a hug. "It's going to be okay," I told her.

"Sweetie." She held my face between her hands. "I know. Everyone's just upset."

Buster hauled himself to his feet and gave himself another shake. The he sat back on his haunches.

"Everyone except this guy," Yasmin pointed out. "He's grinning again. I think he's proud of himself."

"This bad old dog," Mom said. Her voice was affectionate, though.

I rested my head against her shoulder. "This good old, bad old dog."

We all went inside.

Buster lapped at his water bowl for a long time before going to his bed and flopping down.

Mom went to call Animal Control about the raccoon while Yasmin, Sheera, and I helped ourselves to some lemonade. I was horribly thirsty and had a terrible headache.

I poured some lemonade for Mom, then we all sat around for a while, talking about the raccoon and Buster. Mom said that Animal Control would come the next day and put a trap in the yard for the raccoon. Buster's snores fell softly in the room as we talked, and slowly the coil in my stomach loosened.

"Here, Mackenzie, let me see your hands," Yasmin said after a moment. "Pretty!"

"I have such a wide hand," I said, although my mind was still on Buster. "My feet are the same. Short fingers, short toes."

"I love the little dimples in your fingers," she said. "I'll do your nails first; let me get my bag."

She had left a flowered toiletries bag on the couch and brought it over to the dining room table. When she zipped it open, Sheera's eyebrow went up. "That whole bag is just full of nail polish?"

"And polish remover and nail files and other stuff," Yasmin said as she placed bottles on the table one by one. She had three different kinds of clear polish and twenty-eight bottles of color—everything from ballet pink to midnight black to peacock blue to mint to a hideous orange sparkle.

"What's with the brown?" I asked, holding it up.

Yasmin plucked the bottle from my hand and said, "I like to do brown, orange, and yellow around Thanksgiving. Different colors for different fingers."

"What a fun hobby," I said. "I mean, I like to do my nails

sometimes, but this is next level." I held up a classic red. "Sorry to be boring."

"Red is never boring! This is one of my favorites." Yasmin had me lay my hand flat on the table and she started gently filing my nails. "And I wouldn't call this a hobby," she went on. "I mean—I like to do my nails, but it only takes, like, a half hour every ten days. It isn't like judo, or helping my mom at the store." Yasmin twisted open a bottle of clear polish and started on my index finger. "This is base coat," she explained. "It helps the polish stay on."

"You do judo?" That surprised me.

"She's a brown belt," Sheera put in.

"Is that—good?" I asked. I guessed from Sheera's smile that it was.

Yasmin laughed. "Yeah, it's pretty good."

"What about you?" I asked Sheera. "What's your secret hobby?"

Sheera's shoulder lifted, then dipped. "You know all my stuff," she said. "Drawing, manga, playing oboe . . ."

"Singing," Yasmin added.

Sheera blushed.

"And she speaks Urdu," Yasmin went on. She motioned

for my other hand and dipped the brush into the red polish. "My parents never taught me."

"Your mom doesn't speak much, though," Sheera said.

"My mom grew up in Texas," Yasmin said to me. "Her parents had emigrated from Pakistan, but they were all about blending in."

"My mom grew up in New Jersey," Sheera said. "But her parents were more traditional. They insisted that she learn Urdu, and now she's insisting that *we* learn it."

"Like, the written form and everything," Yasmin said. "With the Arabic script. You're so lucky."

"You wouldn't think that if you had to spend every Saturday morning studying," Sheera countered.

"I'm going to learn it in college," Yasmin insisted. "But I'm not going to tell them. Then I can listen in on my dad's phone calls and he won't know." She twisted the nail polish closed and waved me away. "Go forth and dry. Sheera, you're next."

Sheera picked the black polish like I knew she would, and Yasmin got started painting the base coat.

"So, Mackenzie!" Yasmin said brightly. "What's with Orlando?"

"Orlando?" I asked. "Dickens's friend?"

"Yeah," Yasmin said. "I think he's kind of into you."

"What? No," I said. Then I thought it over. "I think he's just super friendly."

"No, I think so, too," Sheera agreed. "He really likes you."

"He's too into *himself* to be into me." My stomach twisted. I didn't want Orlando to be interested in me. Things were already super-awkward with Dickens.

Both girls laughed. "What about you, Sheera?" Yasmin asked. She smiled and looked up at her cousin from beneath her thick black eyelashes. "Are you interested in anyone?"

"What? No." Sheera's shoulders hunched. "No," she repeated, shaking her head.

"Would you even tell us if you were?" Yasmin asked.

"Probably not," Sheera admitted.

"I know who it is, anyway," Yasmin said.

Sheera set her jaw. "No, you don't."

"Okay." Yasmin finished her pinkie with a flourish. "I don't."

"Who do *you* like, then?" Sheera demanded.

"Me? I've only been at this school for, like, five minutes," Yasmin said. "Besides, I have to focus on my grades."

Yasmin's eyes landed on me, and I felt a flutter of panic. I didn't want to talk about crushes. I didn't have a crush on anyone, anyway.

"Hey—we never had that popcorn!" I said suddenly, standing up.

"You can't eat any until your nails are done," Yasmin said. "Let's start the movie. Keep your hands perfectly still for the next thirty minutes."

"You do this every week?" Sheera looked dubious. "This is way too high maintenance for me."

I flipped off the overhead light. Grabbing the remote, I hit play and sank into the couch, glad for the darkness and the distraction of the opening credits.

I wasn't ready to talk about Dickens. I didn't know what to say—I didn't even know what to *think*.

DIY: Making Up

Once again, my brilliant dog plan had turned into stress for my mom.

I heard her on the phone later, first talking to Goldie, who said that the bite wasn't that big a deal since Buster had done it by accident. She still thought we should tell the shelter, but she didn't seem as worried about it affecting Buster's chances of getting adopted as we were.

Then Mom called Zane and told him what Goldie said. I heard him apologize for walking away and Mom said it was okay, everyone had just been upset.

The fact that Zane was so worried about Buster made me like him even more, and now I was really, really worried about what will happen if Mom and Zane ever break up.

And all these thoughts are the reason that I have no idea what the plot of the movie we watched was. In fact, I can't even remember the title. Not that it matters. Sheera fell asleep halfway through it and Yasmin was only half watching the movie while half watching YouTube videos of people making soap.

She says she finds it relaxing.

Maybe Mom needs to try that.

CHAPTER FIFTEEN

"She's here again," Sheera whispered to me the next morning. We were back at the animal shelter, both yawning from our sleepover. Luckily, Sarah had assigned us to organize the pet supplies at the Paw Print Thrift Shop—a little section near the back, where donated pet items were for sale. It was really great for people bringing a new pet home who needed supplies but were on a budget.

"Who's here again?"

Sheera jutted her chin toward the hallway and I saw a short, gray-haired woman walking toward us. Her hair was crisscrossed in braids across the top of her head.

"Oh, hi, Greta!" I called. "Did you just visit Penny?"

Deep dimples appeared in Greta's cheeks as she smiled. "There's just something about that cat," she admitted.

"You should just adopt her," Sheera said bluntly. "Here, I

just found this cute bowl. It's only fifty cents! Get the dish, take the cat, everyone's happy!"

Greta blinked in surprise. "Well, that is cute," she said. It had paw prints around the edge and read GOOD KITTY in the bottom of the bowl.

"It's a set," Sheera went on, grabbing the matching one, which read YUM, YUM.

Greta shook her head. "No, I'm afraid I won't be bringing Penny home today."

"You want to, though," Sheera prodded.

"That's true," Greta admitted, and her eyes glistened a little.

"It's okay," I said quickly. "Maybe you'll be ready one day."

"Why—" Sheera began, but I shot her a look and subtly shook my head. I wasn't sure why she was being so pushy. Sometimes Sheera isn't great at reading people. There was clearly some reason why Greta couldn't take Penny home. Maybe she didn't have enough money. Whatever it was, I could tell that it was bothering her.

But Greta was tracing a finger around the edge of the bowl thoughtfully. "It's hard," she said.

"I know." I tried to make my voice gentle. "It can be a lot of work to take care of a pet."

Greta looked at me. "No—that part isn't hard," she said. "Losing them is. It just hurts too much when they pass on."

Sheera and I exchanged a glance as Greta inhaled deeply and released her breath slowly.

"That's the trouble with love," she said. "It doesn't end, does it? The love just goes on and on, even when the loved one isn't there anymore."

"I understand," I told her. "I'm fostering a dog right now, and I know it's going to be hard when he finds his forever home. And that's a happy ending, right? But I'll still miss him."

Just talking about it made my stomach throb with a dull ache. It was hard to imagine Buster with anyone else. I couldn't really picture it. Whenever I imagined his forever home, I imagined the foot of my bed or next to my mom on the couch.

"Yes, you'll miss him."

I took a breath and forced myself to focus on Greta. "But I won't be sorry that I took care of him when he needed it," I told her. "Even when he's gone."

"Well . . ." Greta handed Sheera the bowl. "That's one way to look at it. Goodbye, girls."

"Bye," I called as she headed toward the front doors.

Sheera placed the bowls back on the shelf. "She should just take that cat," she said. "And stop being so dramatic about it."

"Not everyone is as practical as you are, Sheera," I told her. "Some people are more emotional."

"Here comes your mom," she said, ignoring my comment.

"I love that you have such a great view of the front door," I told her as I stacked the final dog bed.

"Hey, girls!" Mom said. "How was volunteering? This place looks great, by the way. Oh, are these tennis balls for sale?" She started inspecting the large glass jar filled with balls of different sizes. They'd all just been donated by the local tennis club. "Buster could use a new one."

"I already got him one," I told her. "You ready, Sheera?"

"We just need to grab our backpacks," she said. We reached behind the counter while Mom poked around the mini-store. "Oh, these cat bowls are adorable."

"We almost sold them," Sheera told her.

"Someone will snatch them up," Mom said. "Should we go?"

"Let's," I said, and we walked toward the front of the building. "Vera, we're heading out," I called to the adult volunteer as we passed the front desk.

"Okay! Thanks for helping out. See you at Pet-A-Palooza?"

"Definitely!" I agreed. "We'll be here."

"And so will Buster!" Mom said cheerfully.

"You're in a good mood," I noted as we made our way to the car.

"I just got a text from a marketing firm," Mom said with a smile. "I've got a job interview tomorrow."

"Oh, great!" I gave her a hug. "That's so awesome!"

"You're looking for a new job, Ms. Miller?" Sheera asked.

"Yes, but maybe not for much longer," Mom told her as she yanked open the passenger-side door to let me in. "We'll see!"

We all piled into my mom's Toyota and she turned on the radio. An Ashley Violetta song was playing, so she twisted the knob and the three of us sang along at the top of our voices all the way home.

CHAPTER SIXTEEN

"What do you think?" I asked as I held up the bandana.

Mom's eyes crinkled in a smile as she read the message. "For Buster?"

"Yeah, for this weekend," I said.

The bandana read I'M PAWSOME! TAKE ME HOME TODAY!

Mom held her cup of coffee in one hand and picked up another bandana with the other. There were several stacked on the kitchen table. I'd made a few, thinking that the dogs could wear them at the adoption event. I didn't think the cats would be into it, though. "Do they all say the same thing?" she asked.

"No, I made a few 'I'm Un-fur-gettable' ones, too." I turned to Buster, who was happily gobbling up his morning dog food. "What do you think, buddy? Are you un-fur-gettable or pawsome?"

He ignored me, continuing to focus on his breakfast as Mom drained the last of her coffee and stood up. "How do I look?"

"Like someone I would hire immediately," I told her. She had on her black pantsuit and a cream-colored button-down silk shirt. She had styled her normally stick-straight hair so that it was smooth and slightly curled under, and looked very neat and professional. But maybe a little boring. Not that I was going to say so. I mean, the outfit didn't express my mom's personality, but that's what people in offices like, right?

"Are you done?" Mom motioned to my plate, which only had a half slice of bacon left on it.

"Yes, thanks." I handed it to her and Buster, who trotted over to follow Mom to the sink. He sat back on his haunches as she said, "No, Buster. No treats." But I think the only word he understood in that sentence was "treats" because he jumped up and pressed his paws against her leg.

"Oh, crud," Mom grumbled as she put the dishes in the sink. "Down, Buster! Down! Did he get me?"

I inspected her pant leg. "Well, there's a little smudge."

"Is it noticeable?"

"Kind of," I admitted.

Mom sighed in frustration as Buster—sensing that he had done something wrong—rolled over onto his back. She shook her head. "You were very naughty," she informed him. "But you are very dang adorable." She looked up at the wall clock and added, "I'm going to change, and hopefully this won't make me too late. Do you need me to drop you at school?"

"I'll walk," I told her.

"It's cold this morning," Mom said. "Frost came in overnight."

"I'll wear a jacket. Good luck with your interview, Mom." I gave her a hug. "You'll be great."

Mom kissed the top of my head and whispered, "I sure hope so."

I had been planning to see if Dickens wanted to walk to school together, but he was already standing beside his mother's Subaru Outback when I stepped outside. "Hey!" I called, zipping across the street. "You riding? But it's so early!"

"Auditions are first period," Dickens explained. He tapped the window glass, and I saw that his guitar and amp were loaded into the rear. "For the talent show." The skin beneath his eyes was dark, and he was stooped, leaning against the car as if he was tired.

"You okay?"

"Just worried about the tryouts," he admitted.

Dickens's mom stepped out of the house. She looked lovely in a loose dress and her hair flowing down her back. Dickens's mother, Isabela, is a librarian, so she doesn't have to wear suits, like my mom. "Oh, hello, Mackenzie. Do you need a ride to school?"

"I think I'll just walk—not a lot of room with the guitar."

"There's room," Dickens said, and when he looked at me with those warm eyes, I heard myself whisper, "Okay."

Dickens climbed into the front seat and I sat behind his mother. There was just enough room for me to sit comfortably with the guitar sitting upright behind Dickens, like another passenger.

We arrived at Ward about ten minutes before my usual time, and I was surprised at how many kids were already there. Everyone was standing around in clumps on the front lawn, sitting on the planters, hanging out on the steps.

I spotted Sheera standing under a tree with Johanna. I waved, and they both started in our direction. Orlando had been standing near them, and when he caught sight of us, he ran over and helped Dickens pull his amp out of the car.

"Man, you never check your texts!" Orlando cried. "Martin is out sick!"

Dickens's shoulders sank. "You're kidding."

"I'm not." Orlando shook his head. "We are now a duo."

"A duo without a singer," Dickens added.

"*You'll* have to sing," Orlando said, and Dickens just lifted his eyebrows.

"What's up, you guys?" Johanna asked as she and Sheera reached us. "Tryouts?" she asked, looking at the gear.

Dickens shook his head. "No."

Johanna looked confused. "But you brought all your—"

"My stupid brother is barfing all over the bathroom," Orlando explained. "And now we don't have a singer. Unless . . ." He cocked an eyebrow and looked at Sheera, who blushed.

"I don't—"

"Sheera." Dickens's voice was warm, and his eyes were soft as he looked at her. "Would you please sing with us? Just this once? We could just do 'Stand by Me' again. I know that you're uncomfortable, but it would be so . . ."

Dickens is tall, and when Sheera looked up at him, it looked like she was gazing up at the moon. I saw her breath rise and fall. She seemed almost breathless. "Okay," she finally said.

Dickens touched her shoulder. "You will?"

She nodded. "Yes, I will," she said. "Yes."

"Aw, yeah!" Orlando pumped his fist. "Too bad nobody's allowed to watch us because we're going to blow everybody away."

Johanna laughed. "You're that good, hunh?" she asked Sheera.

Sheera shook her head, but Dickens said, "She is exactly that good." He gave her a quick hug, and Sheera's eyebrows lifted in surprise, but she half hugged him back.

"You okay?" Johanna asked me as the guys walked away to put the equipment in the gym.

"Me?" I asked. "Yeah. Fine."

Sheera looked at me, her expression concerned. "You sure?"

My dad once pointed out that if you look at the FedEx logo, there's an arrow between the capital *E* and the *x*. The blank space between the letters forms a perfect arrow pointing to the right. Now when I see a FedEx truck, that's what I see. I can't just see the logo the old way. I always see that arrow.

The way that Sheera had looked up at Dickens . . . it was like the hidden arrow. She had feelings for him. That was the crush she wouldn't talk about the other night. But—what about me?

A little spark of anger rose in my chest, even though I knew it was unreasonable. I hadn't ever said that I liked Dickens. *Did* I even like Dickens? Maybe? But was that gross? He's my friend!

And what was I supposed to do now?

"Hi, sweetie!" Mom called when I walked through the door after school the next day. She stood up from her computer and stretched. "Oh, Sheera, hi! I didn't realize you were coming over."

"We're going to take Buster out," I said. "Maybe throw the ball."

"I'll make you girls some cocoa later," Mom said as we dumped our backpacks near the door.

"Let me just use the bathroom before we go," Sheera said. "Hey, Buster!"

Buster had trotted over to greet us, and I crouched down to scratch him along the back.

Sheera disappeared down the hall and I went into the kitchen to wash my hands and grab a drink.

"How was school?" Mom asked.

"Pretty good," I told her. "Tyler was an idiot in band as usual, but other than that, it was fine."

Mom laughed and her phone dinged. She pulled it out and looked at the text, and I saw the smile evaporate from her face, like breath disappearing from a glass window.

"What's wrong?" I asked.

"Oh." She shoved the phone into her back pocket. "Didn't get the job."

"What? But it went really well!"

"They think I'm overqualified for what they're looking for. Not a big deal." That's what she said, but I could tell that she was disappointed. I gave her a huge hug, and she sighed. "Thanks, Mackenzie. It'll be okay."

Sheera reappeared, and I gave my mom one last look before turning to my friend. "Backyard okay?" I asked.

"Sure—Buster loves it," Sheera said. "Did you guys catch that raccoon?"

"Never came back," Mom said. "Thanks to our guard dog."

"Mom, maybe you should go for a walk or something," I suggested. "Maybe Zane wants to go."

"That's a great idea." Mom nodded. "I need some fresh air."

So Sheera, Buster, and I headed out the back door and Mom headed out the front. Honestly, I think I was even more bummed and worried about the job than my mom was.

CHAPTER SEVENTEEN

"He likes this one," Sheera said as she bounced the ball hard against the brick edge of our patio. It bounced high into the air and Buster raced after it. He jumped, caught it in midair, and took a victory lap around the yard. Sheera looked over at me with a mischievous grin.

I had to chase Buster to get the ball back. "Come on, buddy, give it!" I said, trying to pry it from his mouth just as someone said, "Knock knock" and walked into the backyard. It was Dickens, carrying a box of chocolates with a bow on it.

I felt my face grow hot and I stood up quickly, letting Buster keep the ball. Of course, the moment I lost interest in it, the ball rolled in front of my feet. I tripped on it as I took a step forward, and I straightened up and flashed an *I'm okay* smile, but Dickens wasn't even looking at me. He was facing Sheera.

My brain managed to form the thought, *He's going to tell her what happened with us beneath the tree. And then he'll turn and give the chocolates to me.* I wondered how he would explain it, and I felt a stab of fear.

"These are for you," he said to Sheera.

"Oh, thanks!" she said brightly. Then she turned over the box. "I just have to make sure the ingredients are okay. I can't—"

Dickens nodded. "Yeah, I know, no gelatin. Wali was on cross-country last year; I remember."

She scanned the box and I just stood there, my hands loose at my sides. Then Sheera beamed up at Dickens. "These are great! Thanks!"

"I got them at Sugar's," he explained.

I wasn't used to Sheera and Dickens having a conversation without me, and I felt, like, strangely invisible. I wanted that feeling to go away, and I heard myself say, "That's my favorite candy store!" They turned to me, and I felt my face blush harder. "They have the best stuff!" Now that I wasn't invisible anymore, I actually felt *worse*. "That's really nice of you, Dickens."

"Would you like one?" Sheera asked, holding them out to me.

I stared at the beautiful purple box with the red bow across the corner and I noticed that the lavender shade matched the rims of her glasses. "Maybe later," I said.

"I just wanted to say thanks so much for helping us out at the audition," Dickens said. "We got in."

"Is Martin feeling better?"

"Yeah, he just had a twenty-four-hour bug."

"Oh, good." Sheera nodded. "That's good."

I had the strangest sense, then, that we were all actors in a play. We were saying lines that were written for us, but we weren't being our true selves. I felt stiff, and super-aware of the way my hands were dangling at my sides, and I wondered what the expression on my face looked like. Did I seem normal? Did they? I honestly wasn't sure what any one of us was really thinking.

Dickens looked up at the trees, his brown eyes tracing the path of a yellow leaf as it fell, twirling, toward the grass. "Sheera, we were hoping . . . would you sing with the band again? You're really much better than any of us. You make us sound good."

Sheera looked down at the small box in her hands. "I don't know."

"Okay . . . well . . . think about it." Nodding, Dickens flashed me a smile, then picked up the ball. He threw it, and Buster raced across the lawn. "See you," Dickens said as he headed the other way, toward the gate.

I looked at the yellow leaf where it lay perfectly still against the browning grass. The sky was gray and the cold, which hadn't bothered me before, now seemed to sink through my jacket and into my skin, then down into my bones.

"Let's eat these when we go in," Sheera said, peeking under the top of the box at the chocolates nestled like jewels in their golden organizer. "They look so good!"

"Yeah." My word seemed to fade on the cold fall air. "They look good, Sheera."

Sheera's smile dimmed a little and she shut the box. "I don't know if my parents will let me join the band."

My heart leaped a little and I was embarrassed by my own jealousy. *Sheera's a great singer! She should be in the band!* I thought. And I also thought, *Oh, thank goodness.* "Why not?"

She looked up at me. "If I were Yasmin, it would be no big deal. But her parents are different."

"Very different," I said.

"They're not religious," she said.

"Do you consider yourself religious?"

"Yeah. I am. But I'm different from my parents. They're religious, but they're also . . . cultural. You know, we're Americans, but my parents keep some of those traditional Pakistani ideas, even though my mom grew up in New Jersey. They're not like Yasmin's parents. They're . . ." She sighed instead of finishing the thought. "Still, I'm so glad that Yasmin and I feel like cousins again."

"Me, too."

"No, I mean—thanks. I was kind of a jerk and I didn't want to listen. I didn't believe she'd changed. But she has." Sheera shook her head. "You're nicer than me, Kenzie." Her voice was soft, but the words felt like a knife and I let out an ironic little laugh. Sheera had no idea how mean I really was, how jealous. I still wanted to snatch away that box of candy that should have been for me. I still wanted her to stay home and sing in her bedroom.

"No, I mean it," she insisted. "Really. I want to be more like you."

"No, you don't."

"I do. I want to be nicer."

I didn't want to argue. I didn't want to have to explain why I was horrible. "You're nice, too, Sheera."

"Let's eat one." She opened the box again and held it out. My fingers hovered over the chocolate globes. One had a sprinkle of pink sugar on top. "What do you think this is?"

"Could be anything," she said.

I took it between my finger and thumb, and she chose the one beside it and took a nibble. "Hm," she said. "Some kind of chocolate minty stuff inside."

I took a bite of mine. The chocolate was hard but silky, and it melted on my tongue as liquid raspberry oozed out. "Berry," I said, shoving the rest of the bite into my mouth before it dribbled everywhere. "Mmm."

Sheera finished hers, too. "Too bad they aren't big enough to share," she said.

Buster—who had been investigating the far end of the fence—trotted over and sat up on his hind legs like a gopher. "These are not for you, buddy," I told him. "No chocolate for dogs."

"You can't have everything," Sheera told him.

Buster seemed to understand what she said and went

to claim his ball. He couldn't have what he wanted, so he went and got something else.

You can learn a lot from a dog, I thought.

"Hey, Poppy!" I said as the door opened to reveal my smiling grandfather. The house behind him smelled like oatmeal cookies.

"Ah! What a treat on a Wednesday!" Poppy said. "I wasn't expecting you until tomorrow."

"Is it okay if Buster comes in? I know you're allergic."

"Oh, I can't imagine he'll bother me much if he only stays for a little while." Poppy patted Buster's head, and his stumpy tail wiggled.

As soon as Sheera had left for home, I'd texted Mom to let her know I was heading over to Poppy's. I'd just felt like my day needed a reset.

"How'd the mosaic table turn out?" I asked him.

"Let me show you!" Poppy led me and Buster to the rear patio, where the small round café table stood. The colors were surprisingly vibrant against the black iron of the table and matching chairs. I traced my fingertip across a broken sunflower. "That was one of your grandmother's favorite plates," he said. "It got a dreadful chip one night at a barbecue, but she could never bear to throw it out."

"It's nice you found a use for it," I said as Buster sniffed at the base of a bush and then crouched in the grass. A moment later, a rabbit streaked past him. Buster stood up in surprise, but when I called his name, he came right to me and sat. Luckily, I had a few treats in my pocket, so I gave him one.

"What a good boy!" Poppy said.

"It's funny—he really goes after squirrels—and you should have seen him with this raccoon the other day—but he just seemed interested in that rabbit. He didn't seem to want to chase it." I slid onto the black wrought iron café chair, and Poppy sat down across from me, resting his arm against the table.

"We never know what goes on in anyone's mind, do we?" Poppy asked, stroking Buster's fur. "What do we know about his old home?"

"Hardly anything," I admitted.

"Well, maybe he shared it with a rabbit for a while," Poppy suggested.

That hadn't occurred to me. Now I realized that Buster had been loved, and he had been loved for years. When I thought about his life, I always thought about the part right before he came to us. The part when he was stuck in a garage, like an old bicycle or a broken bookshelf. And I worried about his future—imagining him stuck in one of the large enclosures at the shelter. But I never thought about those times when he was comfortable and treated with the care he deserved.

"It's so nice to have a pet." Poppy's voice was thoughtful. "Alyce has the dearest cat. Selma. And I don't seem to be allergic to her at all."

"You went over to Alyce Allington's *house*?" I asked.

"She invited me over for tea last week. She has a lovely, cozy house, and her partner, Desiree, was delightful." Poppy smiled at me. "Friends are a treasure."

"They can be," I agreed.

"Miss Mac, I know you worry." Poppy studied my face, and for a moment I wondered if he could see deep inside me. Could he tell that I was thinking about Dickens and Sheera, about what would happen if they had feelings for each other?

"I—"

"But I don't worry at all," he went on, "because I know Buster will find a good home. Personally, I'm really excited for this weekend!"

That last sentence settled on me like a weight. I hadn't really been thinking about the fact that Pet-A-Palooza was just a few days away. Buster would have to leave us, whether he found a home or not.

"You've already done so much for him," Poppy went on. "As far as Buster's concerned, you've changed the whole world. Look at how happy he is!"

Buster, as if to prove my grandfather right, was wiggling on his back, snuffling the grass.

"You're right, Poppy," I said softly. "I'll try not to worry about him."

A wave of disappointment mixed with relief lapped at my toes. My grandfather hadn't read my thoughts or seen deeply inside me. He wasn't wrong about my feelings, exactly—of course I cared about Buster—but he hadn't guessed all of it. And how could he? People aren't mind readers.

That's what makes everything so hard. You have to talk about stuff . . . and sometimes you just can't manage it.

"These were good." I took the last bite of my taco.

"Comfort food," Mom said. I think I might have mentioned that my mom cooks almost everything in a Crock-Pot, and taco filling is her specialty. "You done?"

"I'll get it," I said, taking her plate and stacking it on top of mine. I put our glasses on top and went to the kitchen. I placed the plates on the counter to load the dishwasher. I had to make a little room on the bottom, so I re-sorted a few things and then reached for the plates. My hand knocked them, and a glass fell onto the vinyl floor, shattering.

"Buster, no!" I shouted as he came racing in to see what was wrong. "Mom, get him!"

"You broke something?" Mom asked as she grabbed Buster by the collar.

"Yes, obviously," I snapped. I stood there, staring at the glass scattered across the floor in sections and fragments. Broken apart, smashed everywhere, a mess.

Mom's voice took on an edge. "Well, go get a broom, Mackenzie, don't just stand there."

I stomped over to the rack inside the basement door, where we keep the mops and brooms. I grabbed the small hand broom and dustpan.

"Be careful," Mom said as I was sweeping up the chunks and shards and, of course, a tiny sliver sliced the tip of my ring finger and I started to cry. But not a little cry. I *howled.* I wailed, with tears pouring down my face—that kind of cry where you can't catch your breath, where you feel like the tears will strangle you. Buster came over to lick my cheek but I pushed him away. I didn't want him to cut his paws on the glass.

"Oh, Mackenzie, what is it? What's wrong?"

I held out my finger, and Mom said, "That's hardly anything. It isn't even bleeding."

"Why did you ask if you don't care?" I wailed, tears still streaming down my face.

"Why are you being so *unreasonable?*"

"Because *I am being unreasonable*, okay?" I shouted. "I get to be unreasonable sometimes! I had a bad day!"

Mom's eyes flashed. "Well, I *also* had a bad day and *I* can be unreasonable, too!" she shouted. "Guess what? I'm not helping you! Come on, Buster." She picked him up and stalked back into the living room, leaving me in the kitchen to feel sorry for myself.

I sat on the floor crying for a little while, then stood up.

Slowly, I swept the chunks of glass into the dustpan. I did everything carefully and deliberately, forcing myself to think about every movement. *When you're upset, you have to slow down*, I thought.

I felt like I was underwater, pushing against an invisible force all around me as I placed the broken glass into the garbage. I double-bagged the trash so that the shards wouldn't poke through and swept the floor again, careful to get all the tiny pieces. I carried the black plastic bags out to the garbage bin, making sure to fasten the bungee cords across the top that Zane had added as raccoon protection. Back inside, I placed a fresh garbage bag in the bin and wiped the floor with a damp paper towel to make sure I had gotten all the little bits of glass. I finished loading the dishwasher, washed my hands, and went to sit on the couch next to my mom and Buster.

"I'm sorry," I said.

Mom put down her book. "I know. Me, too." She held out her arm and I leaned against her. Her breath was warm against the top of my hair, and her arm curled around me. She smelled like my mom—and like tacos and perfume and a trace of Buster.

Sometimes I forget that Mom's not a mind reader any more than Poppy is.

"I think I might have a crush on Dickens," I said, and instantly wished I could pluck the words out of the air and stuff them back into my mouth, like chocolate truffles.

"Ah." My mom's chest vibrated against my cheek. "Does that feel weird?"

"It feels *terrible*."

Mom twirled her finger around the end of one of my locks of hair. "And how does he feel?"

"I think . . ." I had to close my eyes. "I think he likes Sheera. And I think she likes him."

"Ohhhhh." The word was like a sigh, and I felt her whole body sink with it. "It's complicated."

"It would be complicated *anyway* because we're friends," I told her. "Really old friends. And now with this situation, it's even worse because Sheera's my best new friend." I looked up at her. "How can I stop feeling this way?"

"I . . ." Mom pressed her lips together and gave her head

a little shake. "I don't know how to stop feeling things." She squeezed my shoulders. "All I know is that feelings pass. They're like weather. They can hit you like a storm and rain and rain, but eventually . . . the rain ends. The weather changes."

"I feel like a bad person," I admitted.

Mom gazed down at me, tucking my hair behind my ear. "You're a good person," she said. "You don't have to have perfect thoughts and perfect feelings all the time. Just do your best to be kind. But even if you were a bad person? I would still love you."

I gave her a kiss on the cheek. Then I reached across her lap to pet Buster, who licked my hand. "Like Buster."

"Like Buster," she agreed.

And like Dickens's family loved Milton, and like Sheera and Yasmin loved each other, I realized. Perfectly imperfect people whom we perfectly imperfectly love.

"I'll miss this guy," Mom admitted.

"Don't talk about it," I told her. "Watch TV?"

"Sounds good."

So my mom was the filling in the sandwich as Buster and I leaned against her sides, and we all watched a ridiculous baking show. And, amazingly enough, the storm of sadness did begin to calm down and slowly move away, trailing just wisps of dark cloud. I knew it might roll in again, but for now, there was peace.

CHAPTER EIGHTEEN

"Mackenzie, do you have any more of those dog scrunchie toy things?" Yasmin asked as the wind whipped her hair across her face. "Ag! Bbbbpph!" She liberated her hair from her lip gloss with her lacquered nails, then went on as if nothing had happened. "The stall needs a restock of toys." She held out her arms and I gave her six more of my water-bottle and fleece creations. I didn't have time to laugh about her hair, which was still being carried every which way. *That's what you get for being glamorous at a pet adoption event,* I thought with a smile.

"Thanks! These are selling like crazy." Yasmin grinned. "Tariq insisted that I mark up the price by two bucks and remind everyone that every dollar goes to help the animals."

"Ever the businessman!" I joked. But I was proud that my toys were so popular.

The adoption event had a carnival atmosphere. Leila had called in a few favors from Poochalicious clients and vendors, and a food truck offering smoothies and other healthy foods had rolled up. Aunt Goldie was standing at an "Ask the Veterinarian" booth, and there were several outdoor pens, some holding rabbits, some holding guinea pigs, and some holding small dogs. Of course, there were a few animals that had to stay in the building—ferrets are a little too good at escaping to trust them in a playpen, and chinchillas are nocturnal—but families oohed and aahed as they passed, and volunteers were showing small children how to ask for permission to touch the animals and pet them gently, all while answering questions about how to care for them.

Poochalicious had put up an awesome makeover booth where dogs were getting bathed, dried, and beautified. They had given makeovers to a few of the shelter dogs but were also offering them—for a donation—to anyone who brought a pet along or adopted a new one. Even Zane was there, handing out refillable water bottles with the Poochalicious logo.

Yasmin and her brother were selling donated dog toys and other items from Hope House's thrift shop—and my homemade toys, too. Sheera was helping her aunt at the makeover booth. Dickens was working with the rabbits, Mom was helping Goldie hand out information at the vet booth, and I was acting as a runner between everyone. Buster lounged in a pen with two other senior dogs. On one of my quick visits to say hi to him, I heard someone calling to me.

"Miss Mac!" My grandfather and Alyce were walking across the shelter parking lot, both smiling. She wore a chunky poncho over a flowing purple batik dress that fluttered as the wind pressed the fabric against her legs. My grandfather was wearing a button-down shirt, khakis, and a green L.L.Bean sweater. It still made me giggle sometimes to think of those two as friends.

"This is wonderful!" Alyce gushed. "Look at how many families are here!"

"I know," I said. "The organizers did a great job. And I let them, for once."

"Oh, I'll bet you had a hand in it," Alyce said, her eyes twinkling.

"So, did you just come to check it out?" I asked.

"Actually . . ." Poppy and Alyce exchanged a mischievous

glance. "I've decided to adopt a cat! Alyce is going to help me choose who to take home."

"You're kidding! That's great! The cats are inside, but I'm afraid there's a little bit of a line to get in. They don't want the animals to get overwh—" A white van with the logo for Channel 22 News rolled up, and I stopped talking in surprise.

"Looks like someone called the media," Alyce said just as Mom hurried over and put a hand on my shoulder.

"They came! Mackenzie, would you run over and let Leila know? I'm going to intercept them." Mom gave my grandfather a quick kiss on the cheek and said, "Hey, Joe. Hey, Alyce! Please excuse me."

"Nice chatting with you, Allison," Poppy joked as we watched my mother dash over to the reporters.

I held out my hands in apology. "Sorry, I have to—"

"Go! Go!" Alyce waved me along. "Tell the people!"

Poppy and Alyce headed to the line to get inside and meet the adoptable animals, and I hurried over to the make-over booth.

"Come on, Bear," Leila said, picking up her Pomeranian. Bear looked smashing with a small pink bow on each ear.

"Showtime." She fluffed her hair and straightened her Poochalicious shirt. The reporters were heading our way, led by Mom.

I hurried off to take a quick tour through the booths, checking if anyone needed anything. I stopped when I came to the pen holding Buster. A woman with straight gray hair and jeans that looked as if they had been ironed was petting him. She had on a crisp white shirt and carried a very expensive-looking purse.

"A senior dog can be a great companion," Sarah was explaining. "Buster here is already house-trained and walks well on a leash. Oh! Here's Mackenzie! She and her mother were fostering Buster. Mackenzie, this is Grace Craven. She's just decided to take Buster home!"

"Take him home?" I repeated. Buster's huge eyes looked up at me and his stumpy tail wiggled. I felt the strangest sensation of joy and sadness swirl through me. "Oh, buddy!" I managed to choke out. "You did it!"

"Hey, hey!" Zane trotted up to us, looking worried. "Um, hi, what's going on?"

"This is Ms. Craven," I explained. "She's going to adopt Buster."

Zane's nervous smile froze, and he looked down at Buster. "You're . . . adopting Buster?"

Sarah smiled. "Would you like to tell Ms. Craven a little about Buster? You and Mackenzie can give her a clearer picture of his personality."

Grace Craven gave me a smug smile and said, "Yes, please tell me more about Buster. I just think it's *so* important to take care of our senior animals, don't you?"

"Uh . . . yeah. Buster's great—he actually doesn't seem like much of a senior at all, once he starts running around and stuff," I told her. Buster sat up on his hind legs and I laughed. "And he's very smart."

"Yes, but he can get into things," Zane added. "He got into the trash and Mackenzie thought he had swallowed a hair clip. It cost her mom almost five hundred dollars!"

I smacked my palm against my forehead.

"I plan to crate him when I go out," Grace Craven said.

"Keep him in a crate?" Zane asked. "No—he won't like that. He likes to sit on the couch. He doesn't get into anything as long as you give him his favorite antler to chew on."

"I'm sure we'll be fine," Ms. Craven insisted. She took a step toward Buster, but Zane moved into her path.

"You know that Buster bit someone, right? Me. He bit me."

"I heard that it was an accident." Ms. Craven looked at Sarah for confirmation.

"Oh, it was," I said, stroking Buster's back. "He was defending us from a raccoon."

"Yes, well, you can never be too careful," Zane said quickly. "I just wanted you to know that he could turn aggressive."

I frowned at Zane and shook my head. *What is he doing?*

"Zane, I think my mom needed your help," I said pointedly. "Would you go find her?" He looked confused and then reluctant, but he finally nodded and walked off to find my mom.

Ms. Craven sniffed and took the clipboard from Sarah. "I won't mind having someone keep the raccoons away, I'm sure."

My stomach twisted suddenly. "Would you just wait here a minute?" I asked. "I think my mom will want to say goodbye."

"Isn't that nice," Ms. Craven said as I rushed off.

For some reason, I didn't spot Mom right away. I must

have raced around to every booth three times, but I couldn't find Leila or the reporters, either. Then I realized—they must have gone inside.

I dashed to the building just as my mom and Zane were walking out. "Mom! Some lady is adopting Buster!"

My mother looked shocked and said a quick, "Excuse me," to the reporters, and we both hurried over to Grace and Buster. Mom introduced herself and told Ms. Craven that Buster was a wonderful pet, and then she bent down and put her hands behind Buster's ears to rub them. "Oh, you silly dog," she told him. "I'll miss your face." Buster licked her on the cheek as she hugged him.

Then I got down on one knee. "Buster, I'll never forget you," I whispered into his fur. "You were my first dog." His tongue rasped against my cheek and moved up to my eye.

Mom knelt beside me and wrapped an arm around my shoulders. "You did it, sweetheart. You kept him happy until he found a home."

I kissed her cheek. "*We* did," I said. "And Zane, too." I looked up at Zane, but he wasn't smiling, and his eyes were latched onto Buster.

"Aw, how sweet," Ms. Craven said. "All right. Well, it was nice meeting you. I can assure you that I'll take good care of this handsome fella. Come along, Buster."

"Don't you want to say goodbye, Zane?" I asked.

Zane shook his head. "No," he whispered.

"You don't?" I felt a pang in my chest. I couldn't understand what was going on—I thought he liked Buster! But first he talks about him being aggressive, and now he won't say goodbye?

Zane looked at me, and his voice rose slightly as he repeated. "No. I mean—no, you can't adopt this dog!"

Sarah gasped and Ms. Craven's mouth dropped open. "Why not?" she demanded.

"Because—" Zane looked at me and ran both hands through his hair. Then he looked at my mom, whose eyebrows were drawn together in confusion. *What's going on?* she mouthed. "You can't take him because he's my dog!" Zane finished, and then he knelt on the concrete and Buster raced to him and jumped against his chest. Zane buried his face in Buster's fur.

Ms. Craven's eyes widened and her face turned red.

"Ms. Craven," Sarah said as she spread her hands wide,

"I'm so sorry, but is there any way we could persuade you to look at one of our other dogs?"

"What do you mean?" Ms. Craven demanded. "Of course, I'll look at another dog! I can't take away this man's beloved pet!" Her eyes brightened and she took a tissue from her pocket to dab at them.

"Thank you so much, Ms. Craven," I cried. "And Zane!" Buster jumped on me, then on my mom, and soon we were all hugging and petting Buster, and Zane even gave Ms. Craven a hug before he started filling out the paperwork.

I watched him as Buster wiggled beneath my ear scratches, and I felt like a pothole in my heart had been fixed and patched. Like a major problem was just . . . smooth.

"Come on, Buster," Zane said finally. "I want to pick out a few things for you at the Poochalicious booth."

Mom looked at me and we both cracked up. Who knew that Zane would turn into a pet guy?

I was following them back toward the booth to see if anyone needed anything when a voice near my shoulder said, "Hello, dear."

When I turned, I saw a friendly, lined face framed with white hair pulled into braids. Greta gave me a bright smile.

"Greta, hi," I said. "Have you come to visit Penny?"

"Well, no," Greta admitted. She looked over her shoulder slyly, then turned her dark eyes back to me. "I've come to take Penny home."

"You have? That's wonderful!"

"I've been thinking about what you said," Greta admitted. "About how you can't let the fear of what might happen stop you from loving now. And I realized that I have been. I have been living in fear. But I think that cat belongs with me."

"She does, Greta," I told her. "She absolutely does."

"And your friend who basically told me to snap out of it—she was right, too."

I laughed. "Yeah, she has a way with words." I glanced over at Sheera, who was combing out a black-and-white cocker spaniel's long ear. She felt my gaze and looked up at me. She waved to both of us, and we waved back.

Greta nodded. "So I just wanted to come and thank you."

"I hope you two live happily ever after," I told her. I really meant it.

"Oh . . ." Greta's eyes twinkled. "We will." She turned

and walked toward the shelter, and I felt a hand on my back. It was Mom.

"Look at the good you've done today," she said.

"Well, you did some good, too," I told her. "Your marketing stuff really worked. And Yasmin and Leila and Dickens and Goldie and even Tariq—everyone at the shelter. We all did it."

"We did. We should feel good about it." Mom smiled and gave me a hug. We stood there for a while like that, just giving each other a hug in the middle of the parking lot full of booths and animals. Then I remembered that my friends were there and probably some other people from my school, too, and I took a step backward. "So, we should probably go help some more," I said.

Mom nodded. "There's more good to do."

I decided to check in with Yasmin to see if she needed anything, but when I got near the rabbits, I spotted Dickens standing next to Johanna, who was holding a cream-colored lop-eared bunny. "Look, Zee-Zee!" she cried. "We're going to take home Peanut Butter!"

"You are?" I asked. "But don't bunnies usually come in pairs?"

"This guy gets along with cats," Dickens explained. "And isn't part of a bonded pair, so—"

"So he'll come home and meet Batman," Johanna finished. "Isn't that cool?"

"Very cool. You'll have to send me photos—that rabbit is about twice the size of Batman," I said with a laugh. I knew Johanna's cat was friendly and even-tempered. "You're gonna have fun, Peanut Butter." I gave the rabbit a scratch behind the ears.

"He's very sweet," Johanna's mom said, and I agreed.

At that moment, my mom, Poppy, and Alyce walked through the doors. Poppy was carrying a cat carrier by the handle and Alyce waved. "Come meet Sushi!"

I hurried over to get a look at the kitten, but it wasn't a kitten. It was a large calico cat with green eyes and long hair. "Sushi?" I asked. "I thought you were getting a kitten!"

"This girl chose me," Poppy explained. "Came right up to me and demanded to be petted. What could I do?"

"He was a hopeless victim of circumstances," Alyce said.

"I think Joe has excellent taste," Mom said, and I had to agree.

Sushi let out a meow, and Poppy said, "All right! All right! We'll get you home," and I could see how this was going to go: My grandfather was going to get bossed around by his new cat.

"You have no idea how lucky you are," I told Sushi.

Poppy gave me a quick kiss goodbye and then he and Alyce headed toward her car. I turned back to chat with Dickens, but he was helping Johanna load Peanut Butter into a carrier. Then he volunteered to haul it to Johanna's mom's car, since she was trying to juggle the new litter box, hay, and other supplies while her mom wrote a check to the shelter. I saw Sheera hurry to join them. She grabbed the hay, and I watched the three of them joking and laughing as they walked away. I felt a little invisible, like I had when Dickens gave Sheera the chocolates, but I just took a deep breath and watched them go.

"Ms. Miller!" Yasmin hurried over, waving her hands. "Ms. Miller, the camera crew is leaving; my mom just wanted you to know."

"Okay, let me go say thank you," Mom said, hurrying off.

"Oh, hey, Buster's still here?" Yasmin asked me. "Sheera said someone adopted him?"

"Your uncle!" I filled her in on all Buster's adventures that afternoon, and the way his day was about to end happily in the perfect new home.

"You're kidding!" Yasmin gave me a high five. "Mackenzie, you always manage to get things to work out."

"Not always," I told her.

Yasmin waved her arms around, indicating the booths and shelter and everything.

"I didn't do all this!" I insisted.

"Maybe not, but you hooked my family up with it. This has been great for Poochalicious, too, you know. People are signing up for classes and day care left and right! And you're saving this guy." She bent down and patted Buster on the side. "And you helped Sheera and me, which is huge."

I looked over at Sheera, who was still chatting with Dickens. He said something I couldn't hear, and Sheera laughed. "Yeah," I said faintly.

As if she felt my gaze, Sheera looked up and smiled at me.

"So be happy!" Yasmin poked me in the arm. "You did it! There are no more cats in the shelter, Mackenzie! None! No dogs, either! Every last one found a home! Do you know how many more animals they can help now? Be happy!"

I looked down at Buster, who was sitting and watching the scene. His body is so long that his little rear legs stick out to the side as he props himself on his front legs. It makes him look casual. Around me, the event was emptying out and the shelter volunteers were starting to clean up. I caught sight of Greta and a volunteer with a carrier heading to her car. *Goodbye, Penny*, I thought. *Enjoy the love.*

Sheera and Dickens made their way over. "This was amazing!" Sheera gushed.

"I can't believe how well this went," Dickens added.

"Would you two please tell Mackenzie that she should be proud?" Yasmin demanded.

"You should be!" Sheera insisted. "I mean, you're the reason I'm here, and Dickens is here, and Poochalicious is here."

"Goosie to the rescue once again," Dickens teased.

"You made it work, Mackenzie," Yasmin announced.

"Yeah," I said. I looked from friend to friend and finally felt like smiling. "I guess I kind of did."

"Hah! Look at this!" Mom said, holding up the newspaper at breakfast the next morning. The adoption event was on the front page of the Local section, complete with a gorgeous photo of Leila and Bear. Leila had managed to hold Bear so that the Poochalicious logo was fully visible across the front of her shirt.

"Wow—that plus the piece on the news last night," I said. "Way to go, Mom."

"There's a bunch of photos on the news website, too," Mom went on. "A whole gallery!"

"Everyone's going to be sharing that on social media," I said.

"I'm already on that. And guess—oh, wait." Her phone was ringing. "It's Leila, hold on a second." She touched the screen and said, "Hey! Did you see the paper? I know! You what?"

Mom gave me a little *hang on* wave and stepped out into the garden. I heard her voice going up and down as I poured myself some orange juice and put a slice of bread in the toaster. I heard someone clawing at the front door and looked over to see Buster, with Zane right behind him.

"Hey, you two!" I said, letting them in. "How was your first night together?"

"He took a little while to settle down, but then I let him up at the foot of my bed and he fell asleep pretty quickly," Zane said. "Who's your mom talking to?"

"Leila," I told him. "The post-event recap. Can I get you anything?"

"Think I can have some coffee?" Zane asked as Buster trotted over to claim his usual spot on the couch.

"Mom's already got hers; there's still plenty left," I told him.

Zane poured himself a cup and sat down at the kitchen table just as Mom came back inside. "You won't believe this! Poochalicious wants to hire me to handle social media, PR, and marketing!"

"You mean, like, as a *job*?" I asked.

"It's freelance," Mom explained. "But what I was just about to tell you before Leila called is that I got an email from the shelter last night. They got a grant to redo their social media presence, and they want to pay me to be a consultant!"

"So—two jobs?" I asked.

"Two part-time jobs that I can do from home," Mom said. "Honestly, if this keeps up, I may not need to go back to an office at all!"

Zane held up his mug. "All hail the work-from-home economy!"

"You are not allowed to just hang out in pajamas all day," I told my mom.

"These are lounge joggers," Zane said defensively. "They're very stylish."

Laughing, I gave my mom a huge hug. "I'm so happy," I told her.

"Me, too," she whispered.

It was so strange. Nothing had worked out the way I had expected. It had worked out *better*. Except for the situation with Sheera and Dickens . . . which hadn't really worked out at all. As in, I still didn't know how either of them felt, or how I felt, or what was happening.

But the weather had definitely changed. There might be clouds on the horizon, but for now . . . there was sun.

Mackenzie's Super-Simple Dog Crinkle Toy

Every dog loves a chew toy, and we all have plastic bottles that need recycling. Here's an environmentally friendly way to give your pup a treat!

Materials:

* 1 empty water bottle (completely dry)
* 1 colorful sock (mid-calf or knee socks will work best)
* Scissors
* (optional) A few pieces (about a tablespoon) of your dog's favorite dry kibble

1. Remove cap from water bottle and discard. (The bottle cap could be a choking hazard, and you don't need it for crinkle fun.) If desired, place some dry kibble into the bottle.
2. Place empty water bottle into sock bottom first, so that the top of the water bottle and the top of the sock both face upward.

3. Cut from the top of the sock down, making a few wide strips (about 1/2-inch each), like a fringe. The strips should end at the top of the water bottle.

4. Tie the strips together across the top of the water bottle. Then divide them into three sections and braid. Tie off the ends of the strips at the end of the braid.

5. Making sure none of the fringe gets eaten, enjoy the happy sound of crinkles as your dog chews away!